THE DOG and PONY SHOW

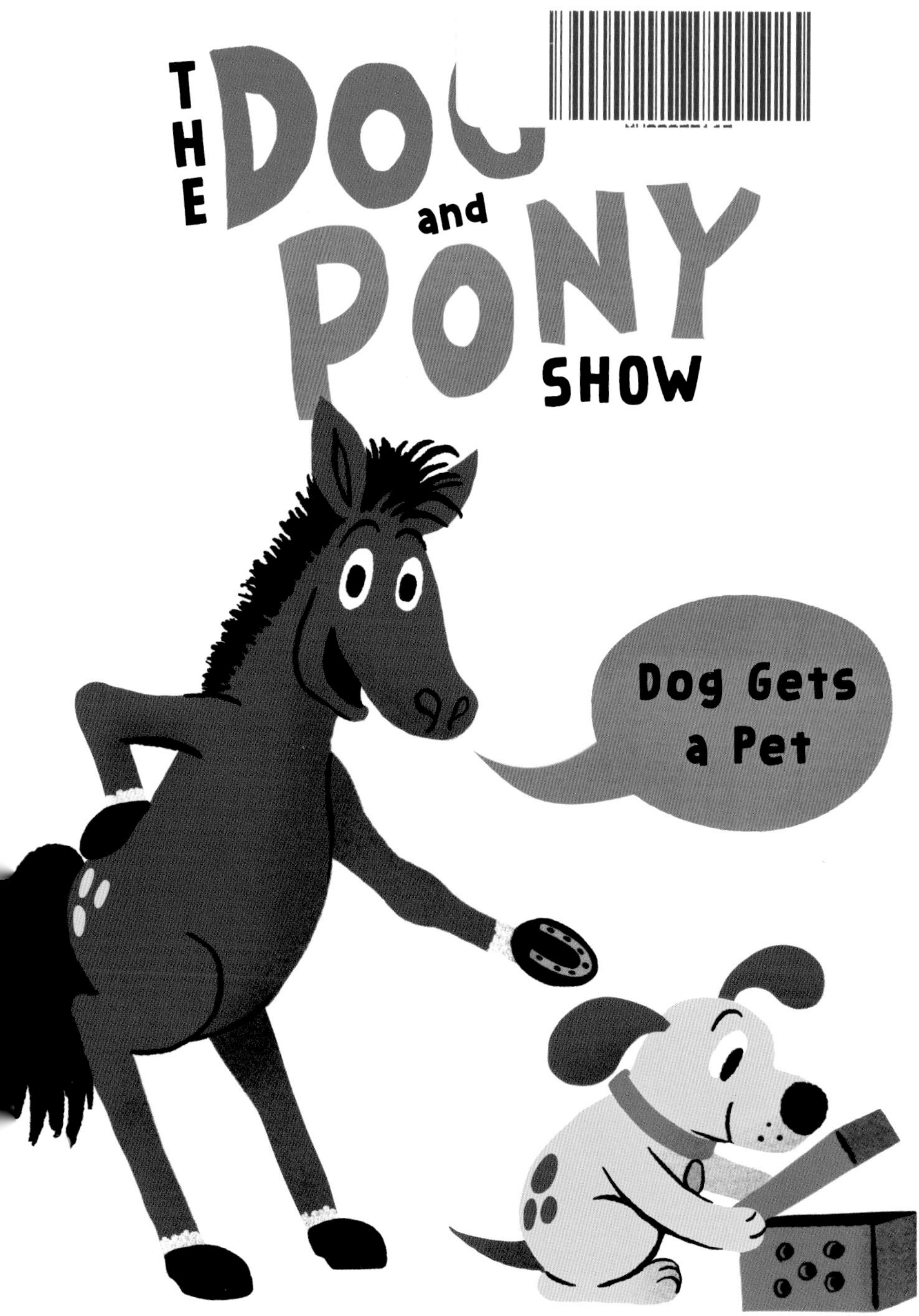
Dog Gets a Pet

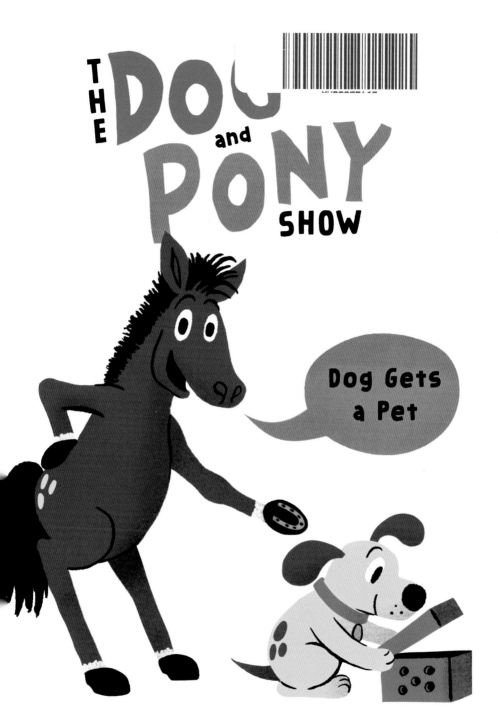

For my brother, Brian, who
loves every pet he gets

SIMON SPOTLIGHT
An imprint of Simon & Schuster Children's Publishing Division
1230 Avenue of the Americas, New York, New York 10020
This Simon Spotlight edition May 2024
Text and illustrations copyright © 2024 by Jeff Mack
All rights reserved, including the right of reproduction in whole or in part in any form.
SIMON SPOTLIGHT, READY-TO-READ, and colophon are registered trademarks
of Simon & Schuster, LLC.
Simon & Schuster: Celebrating 100 Years of Publishing in 2024
For information about special discounts for bulk purchases, please contact
Simon & Schuster Special Sales at 1-866-506-1949 or business@simonandschuster.com.
The Simon & Schuster Speakers Bureau can bring authors to your live event. For more information
or to book an event contact the Simon & Schuster Speakers Bureau at 1-866-248-3049
or visit our website at www.simonspeakers.com.
Manufactured in China 0124 SCP
2 4 6 8 10 9 7 5 3 1
CIP data for this book is available from the Library of Congress.
ISBN 978-1-6659-3912-6 (hc)
ISBN 978-1-6659-3911-9 (pbk)
ISBN 978-1-6659-3913-3 (ebook)

THE DOG and PONY SHOW

Dog Gets a Pet

Written and illustrated by
JEFF MACK

Ready-to-Read *GRAPHICS*

Simon Spotlight
New York   London   Toronto   Sydney   New Delhi

HOW TO READ THIS BOOK

Pony is here to give you some helpful tips on reading this book.

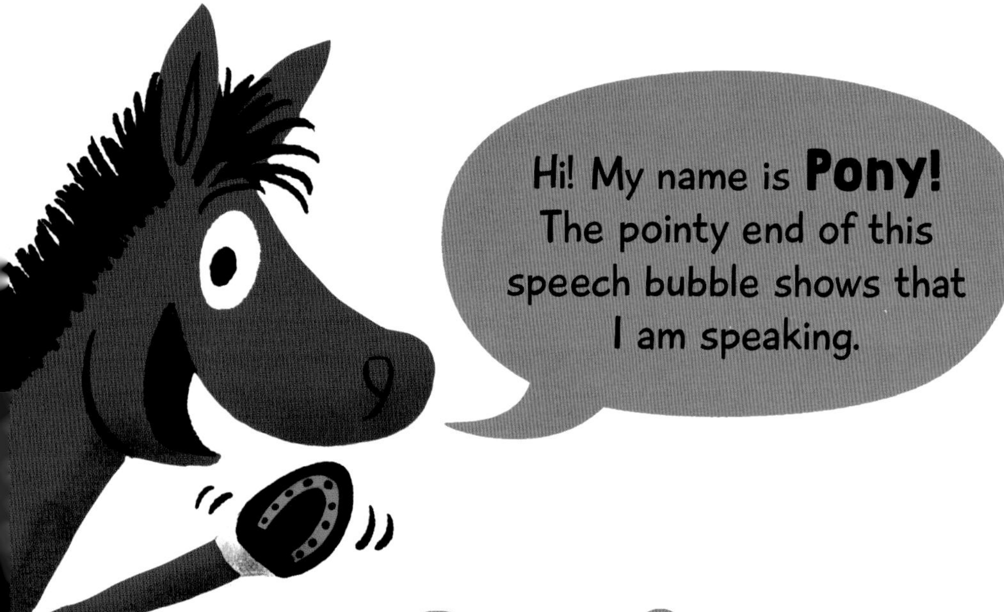
Hi! My name is **Pony!** The pointy end of this speech bubble shows that I am speaking.

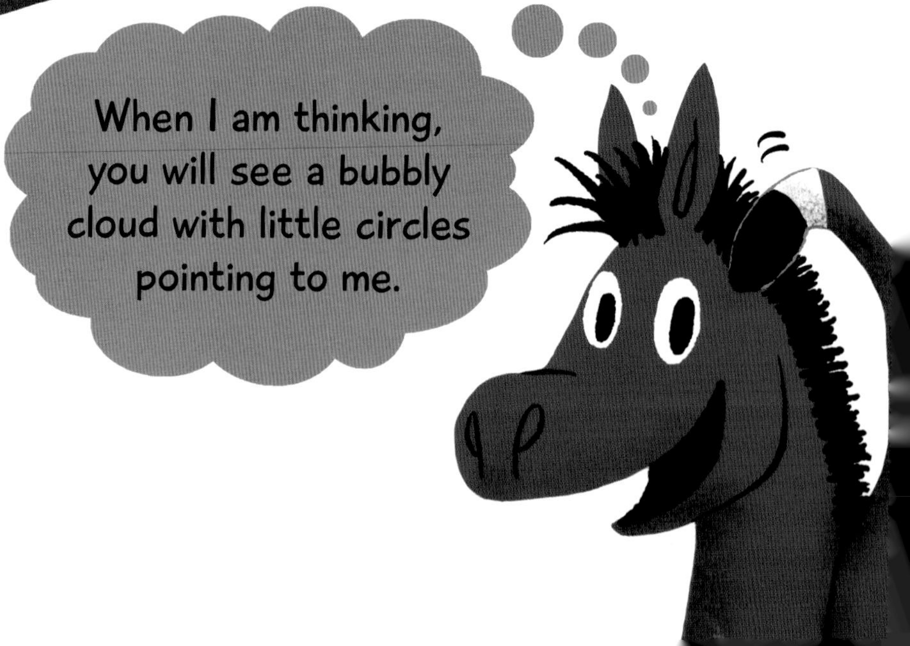
When I am thinking, you will see a bubbly cloud with little circles pointing to me.

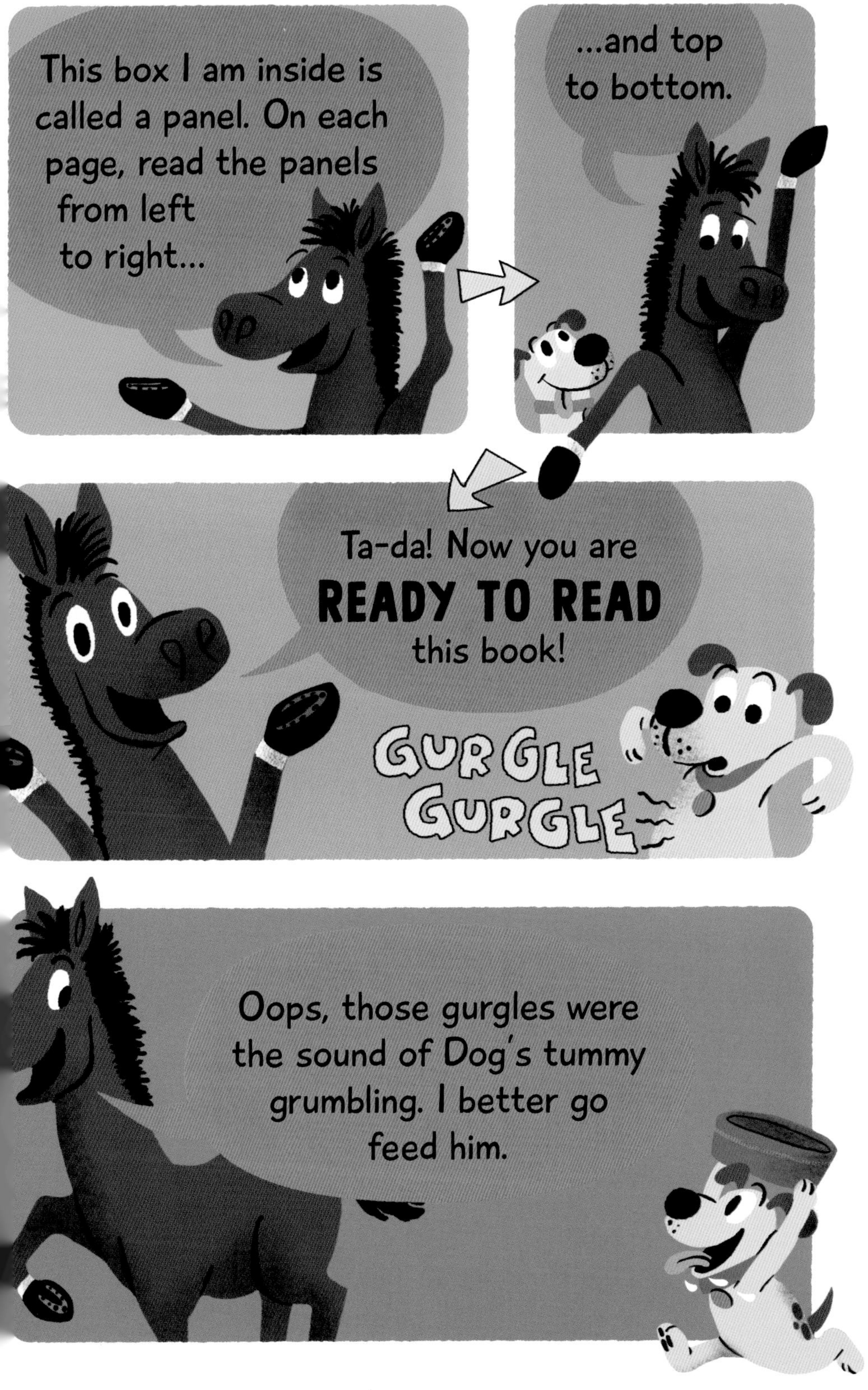
This box I am inside is called a panel. On each page, read the panels from left to right...
...and top to bottom.
Ta-da! Now you are
READY TO READ
this book!
GURGLE
GURGLE
Oops, those gurgles were the sound of Dog's tummy grumbling. I better go feed him.

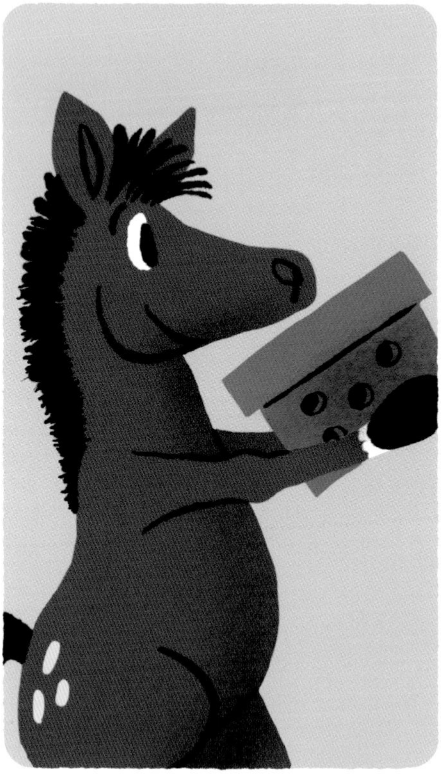
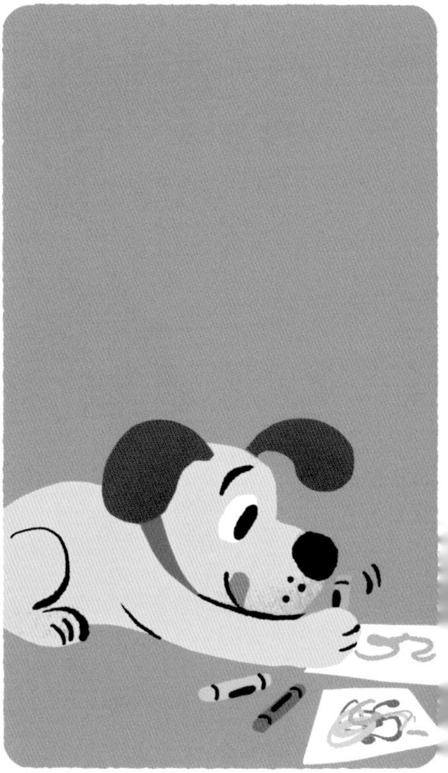
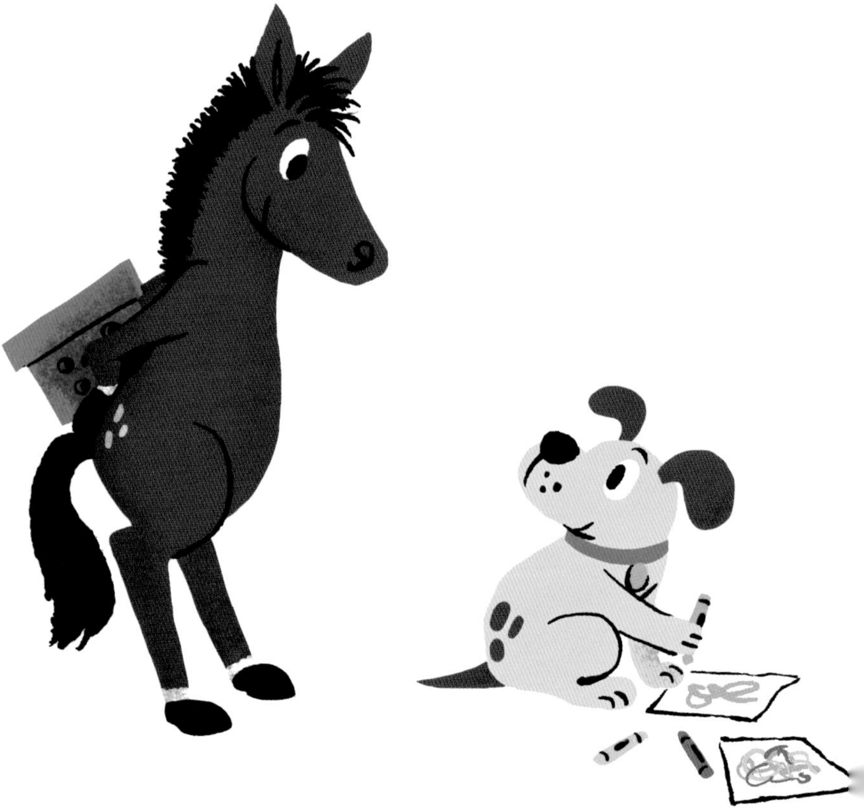

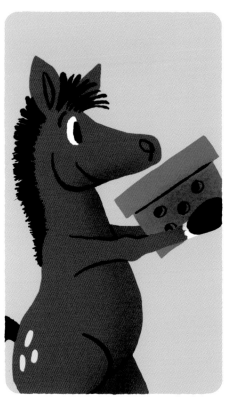

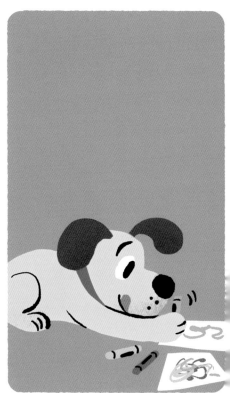

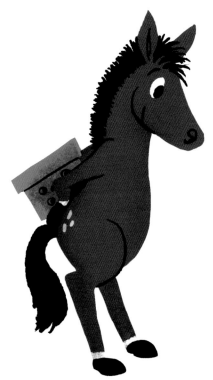

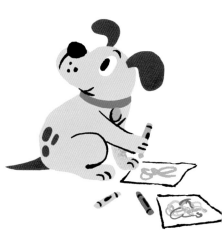

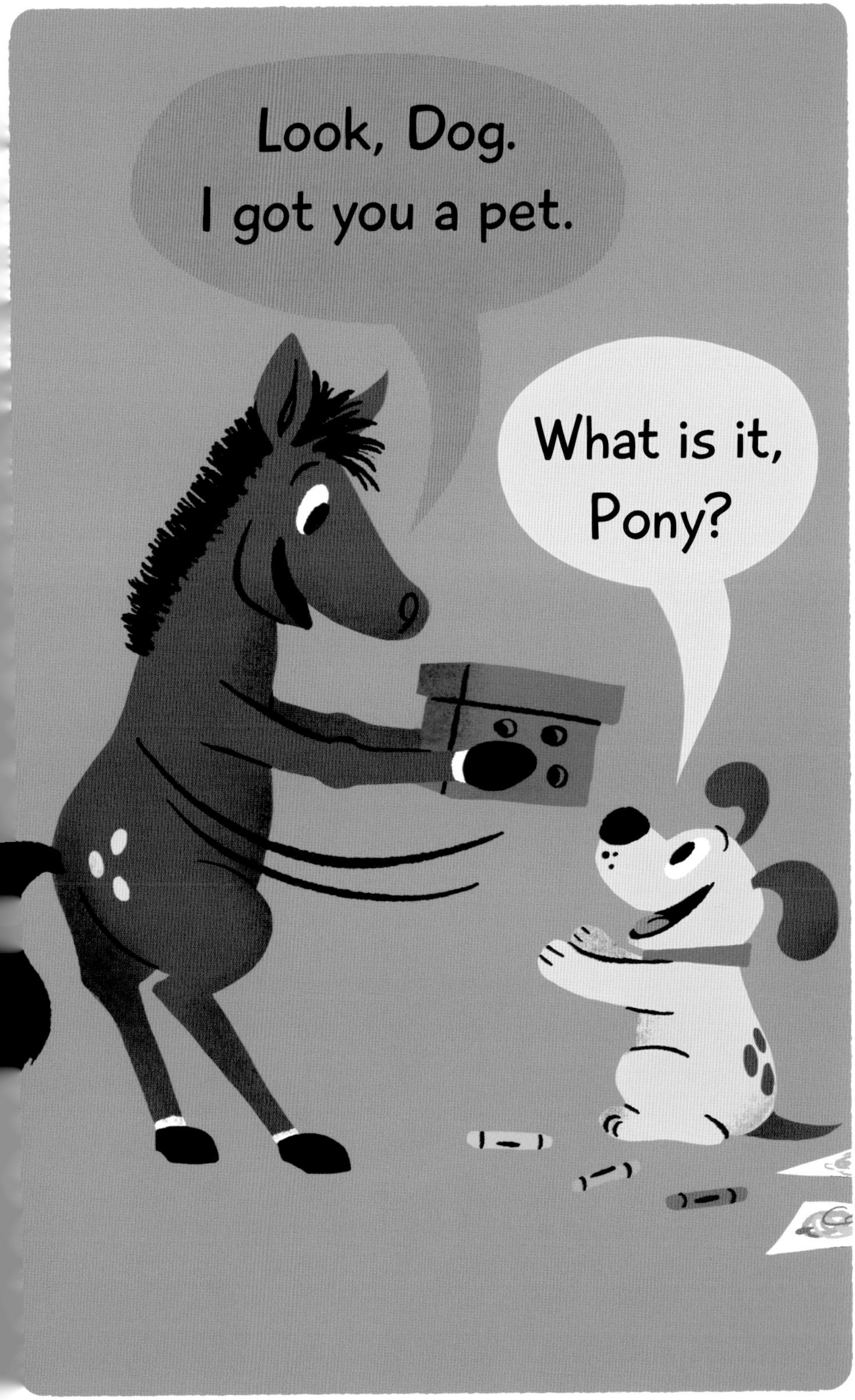
Look, Dog.
I got you a pet.
What is it,
Pony?

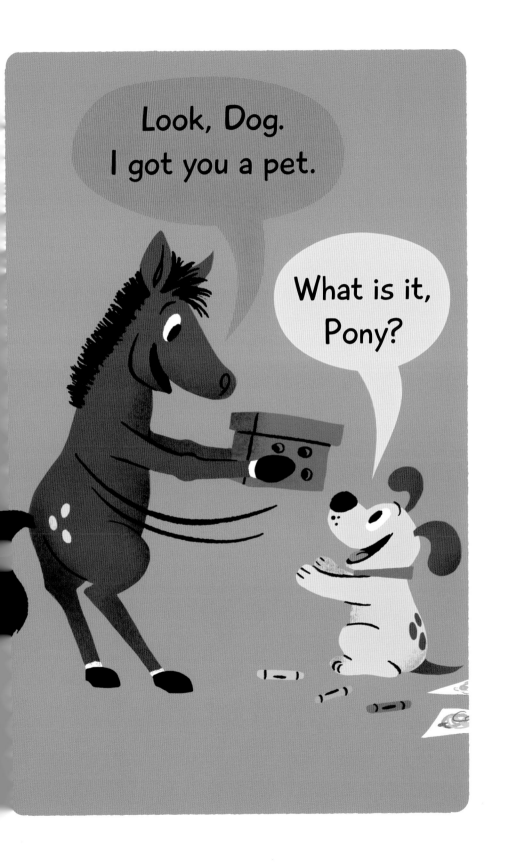

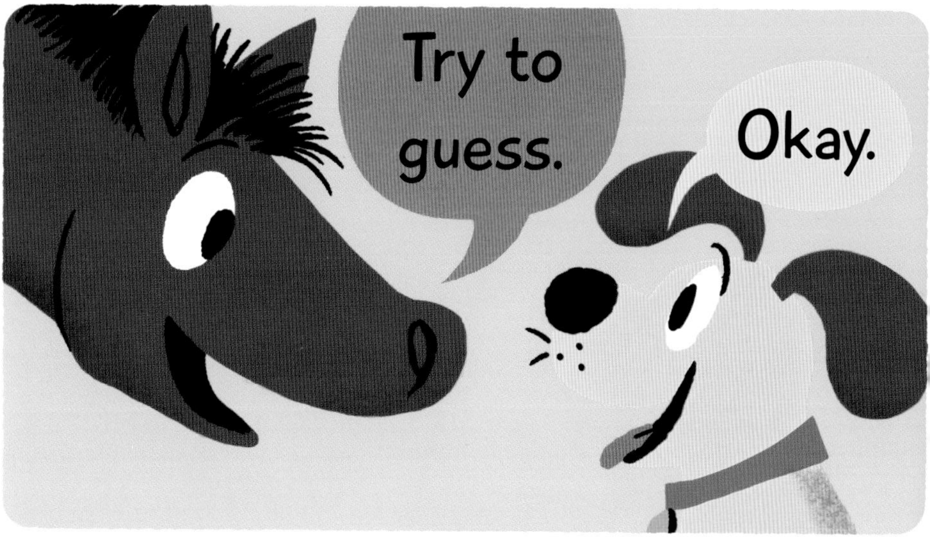
Try to guess.
Okay.

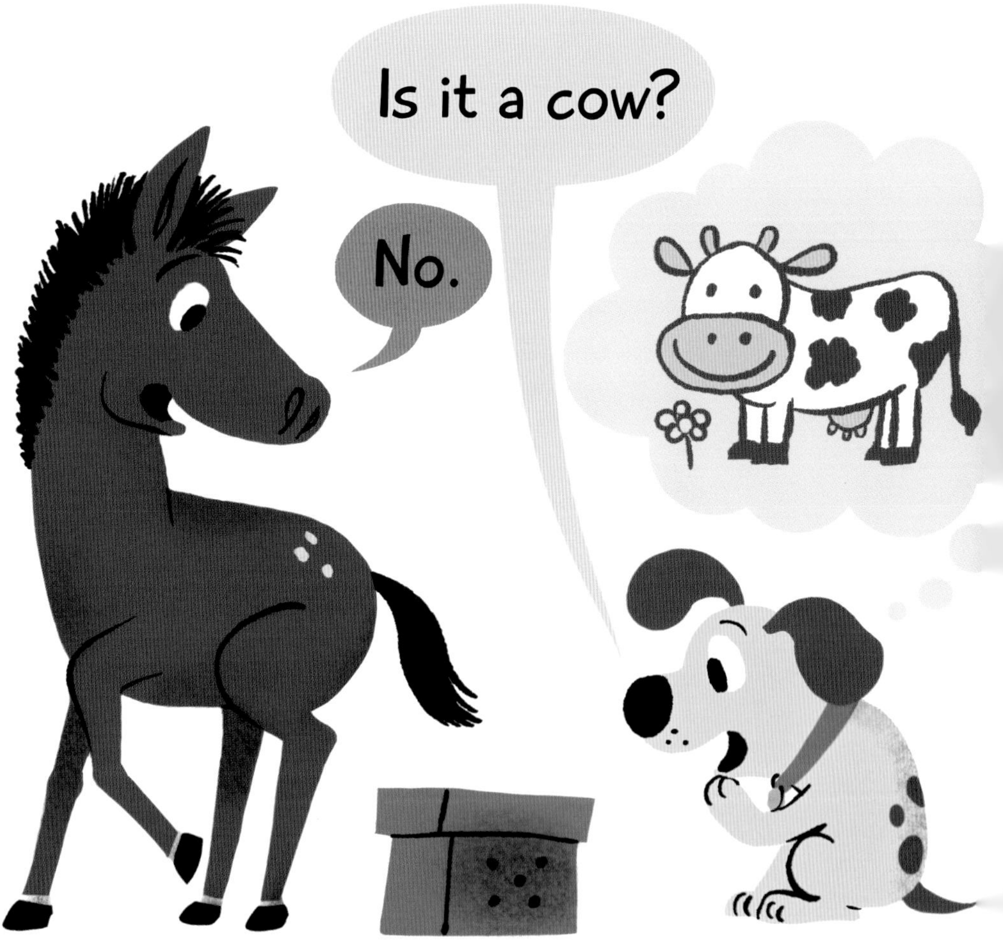
Is it a cow?
No.

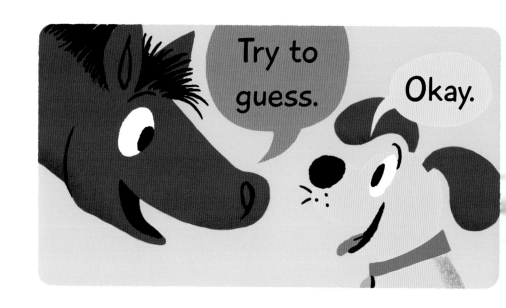

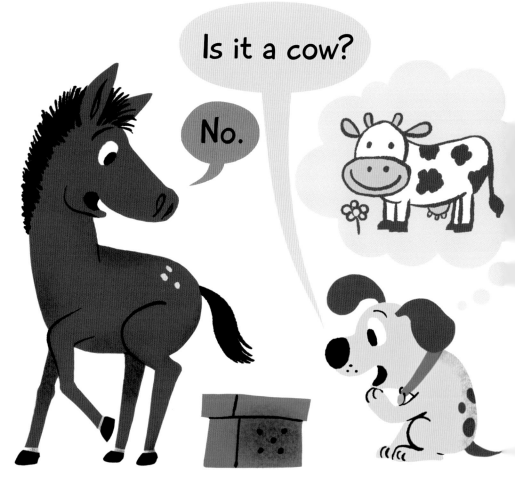

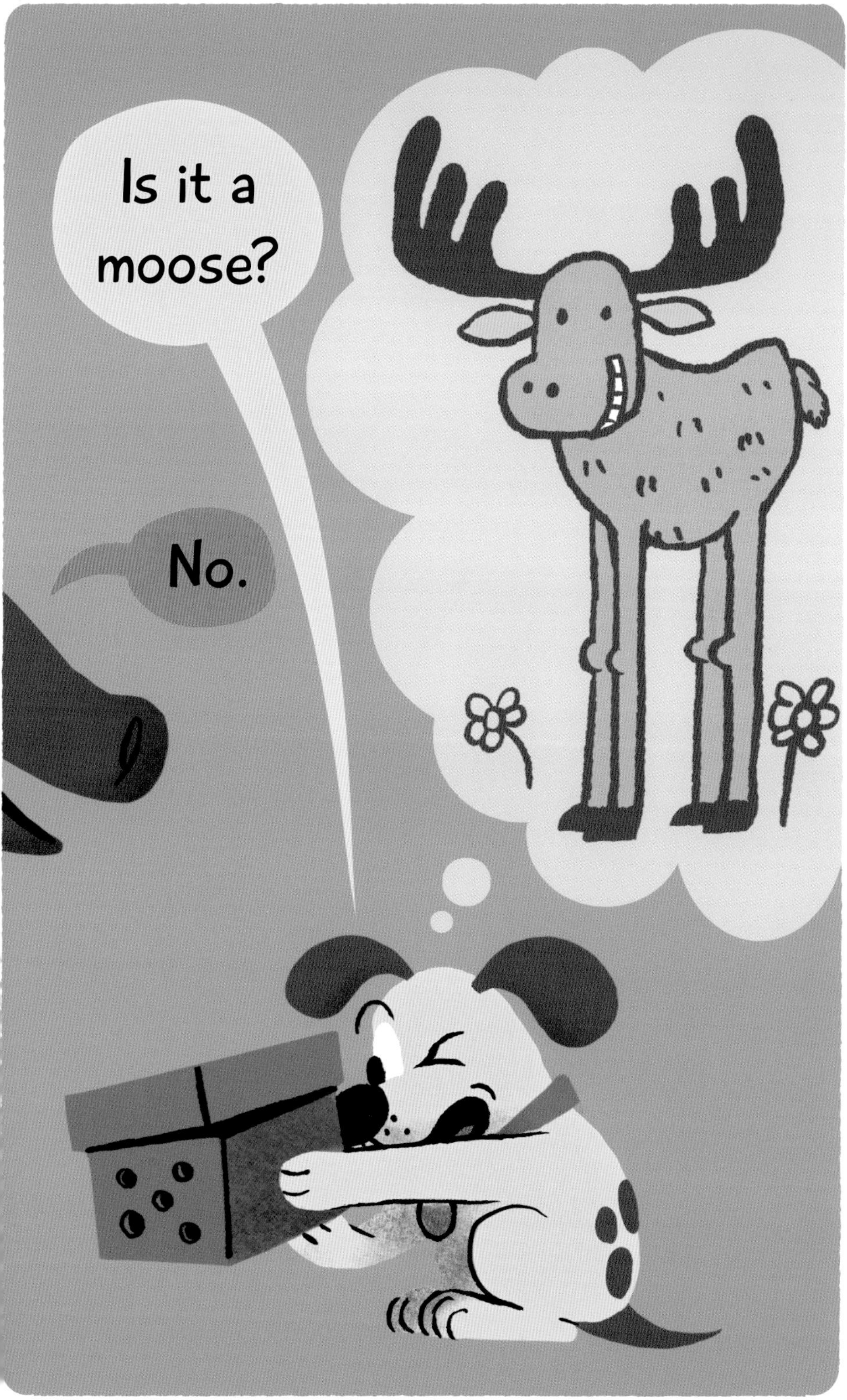
Is it a moose?
No.

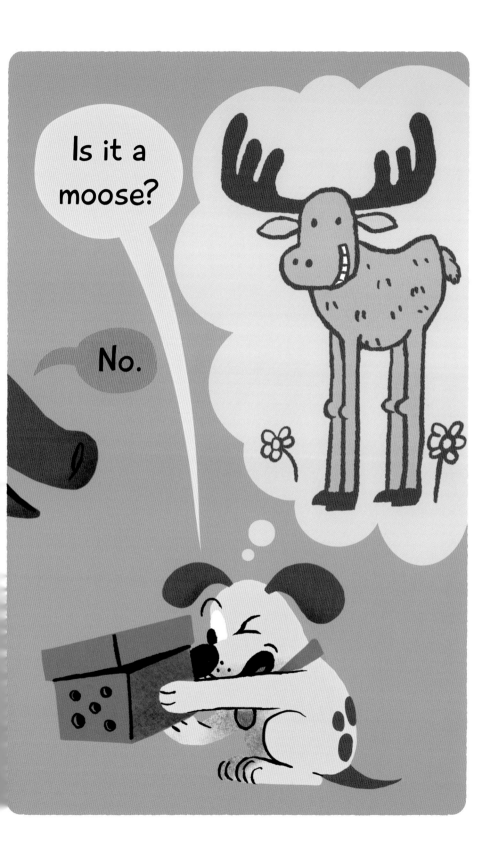

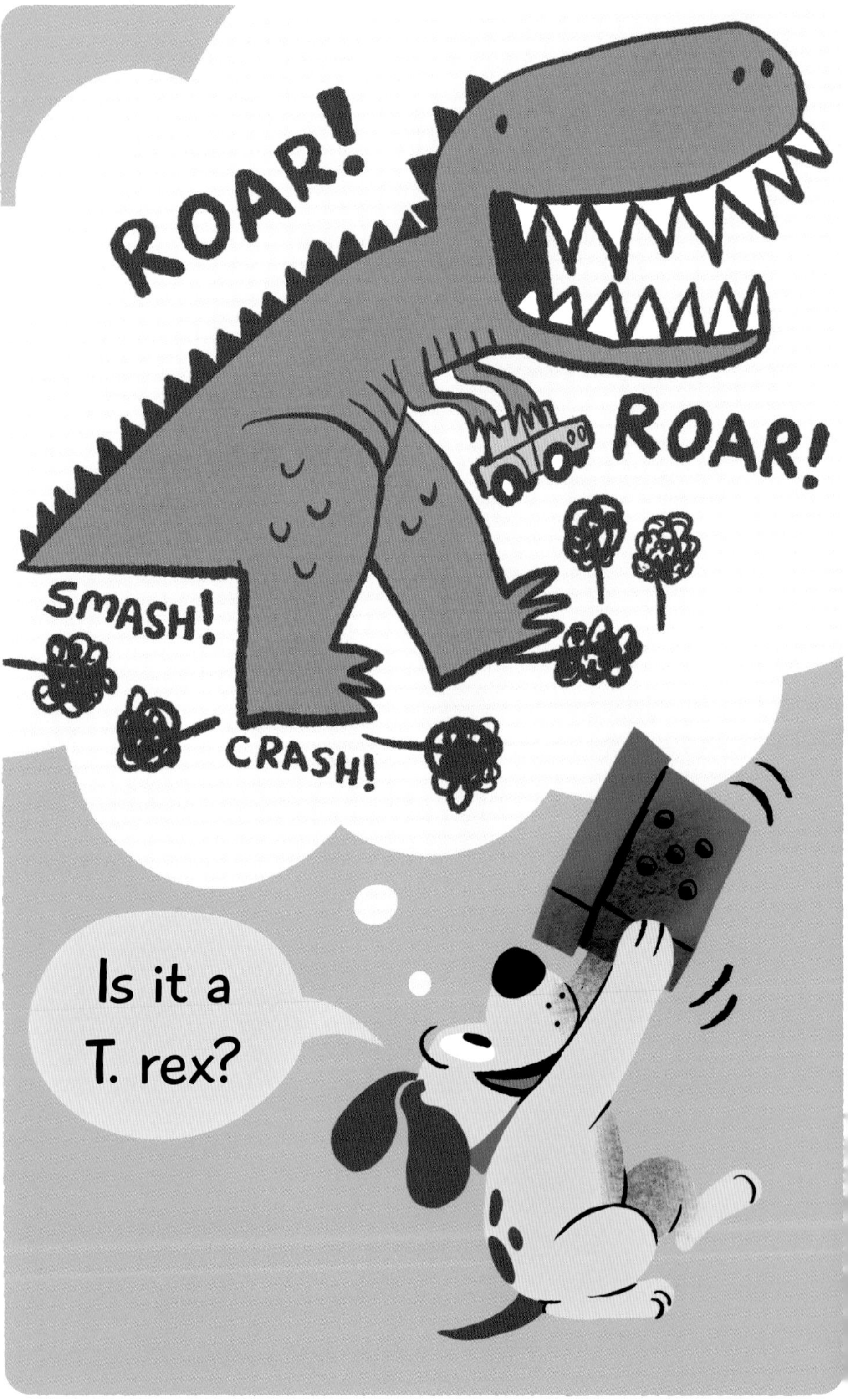
ROAR!
ROAR!
SMASH!
CRASH!
Is it a T. rex?

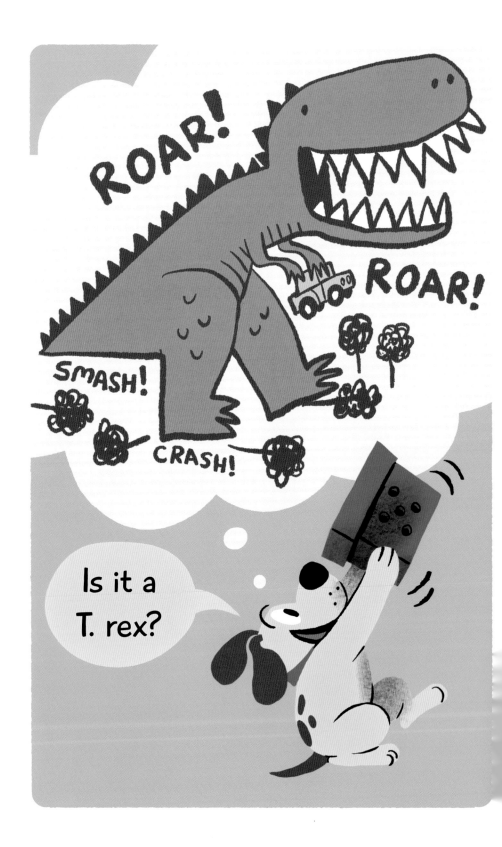

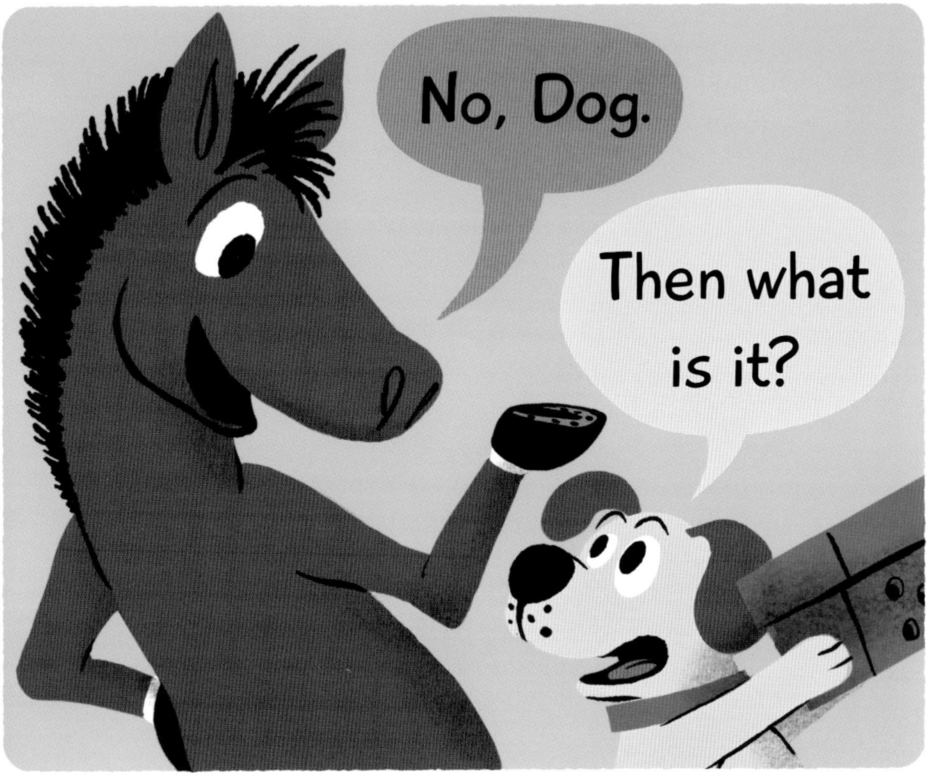
No, Dog.
Then what is it?

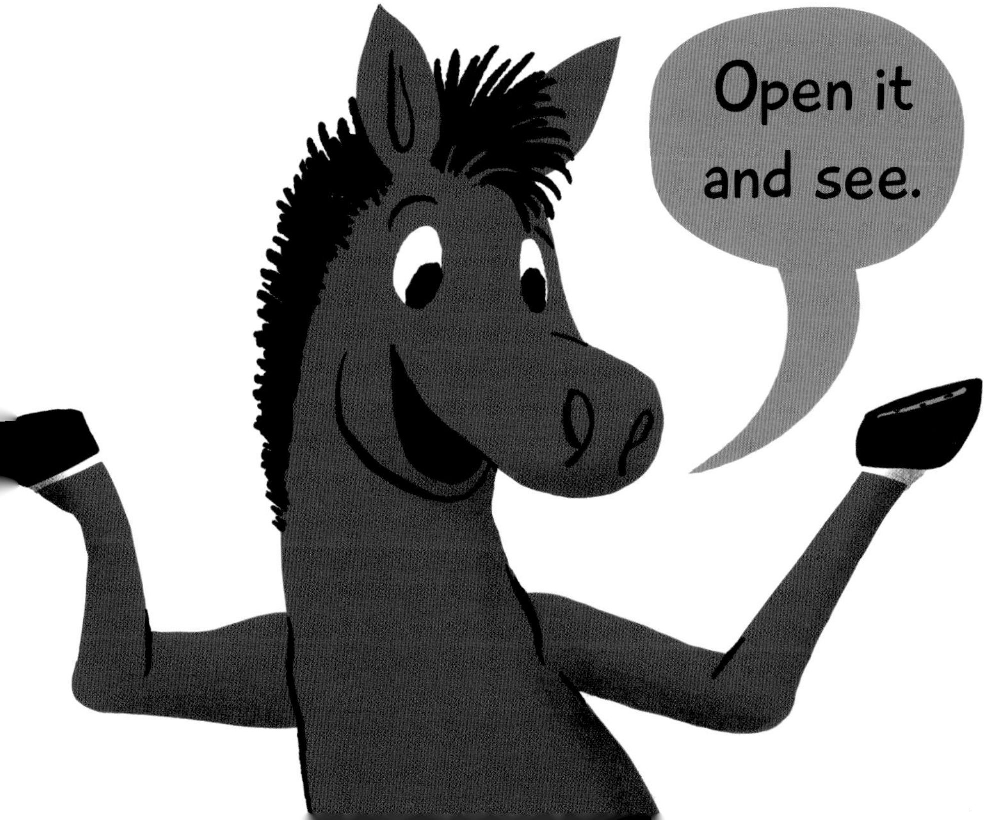
Open it and see.

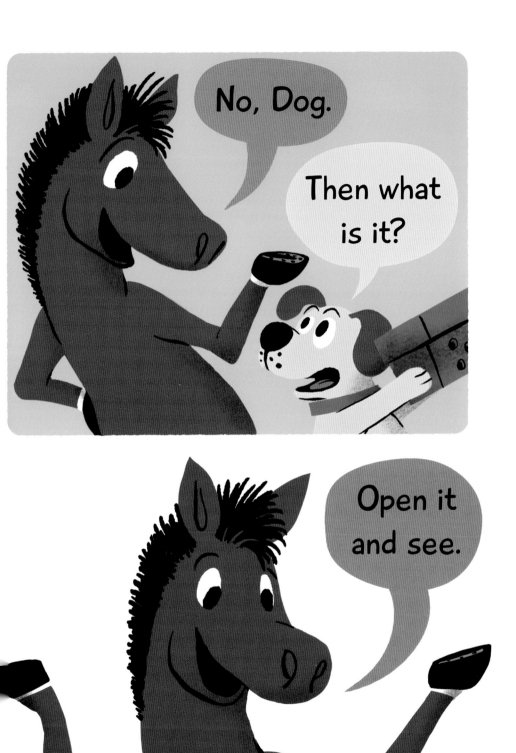

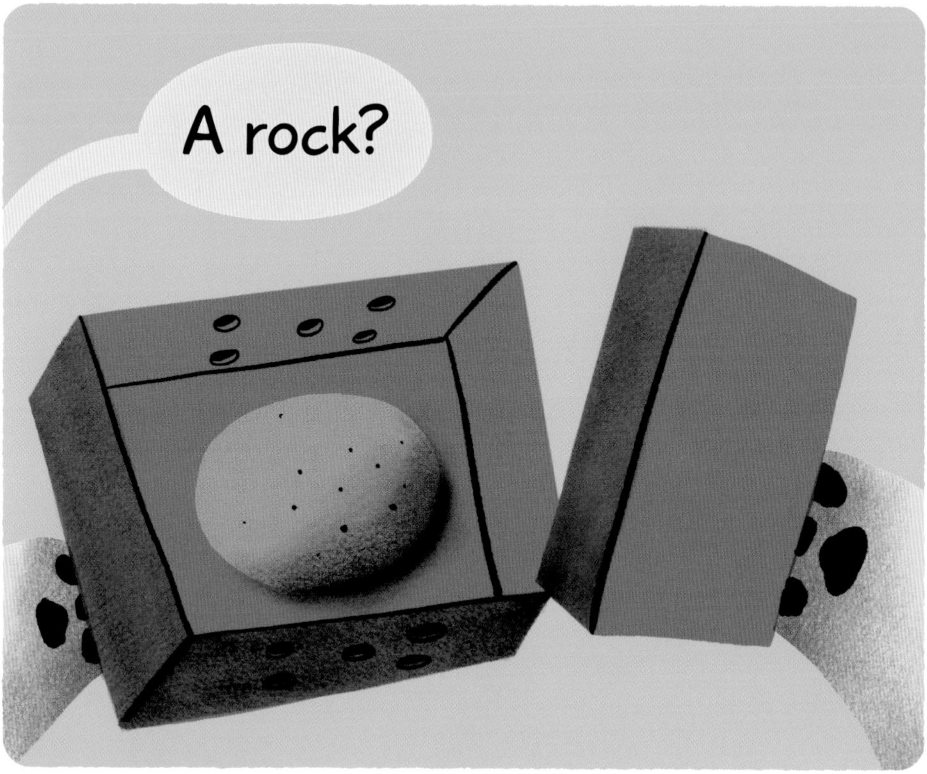
A rock?

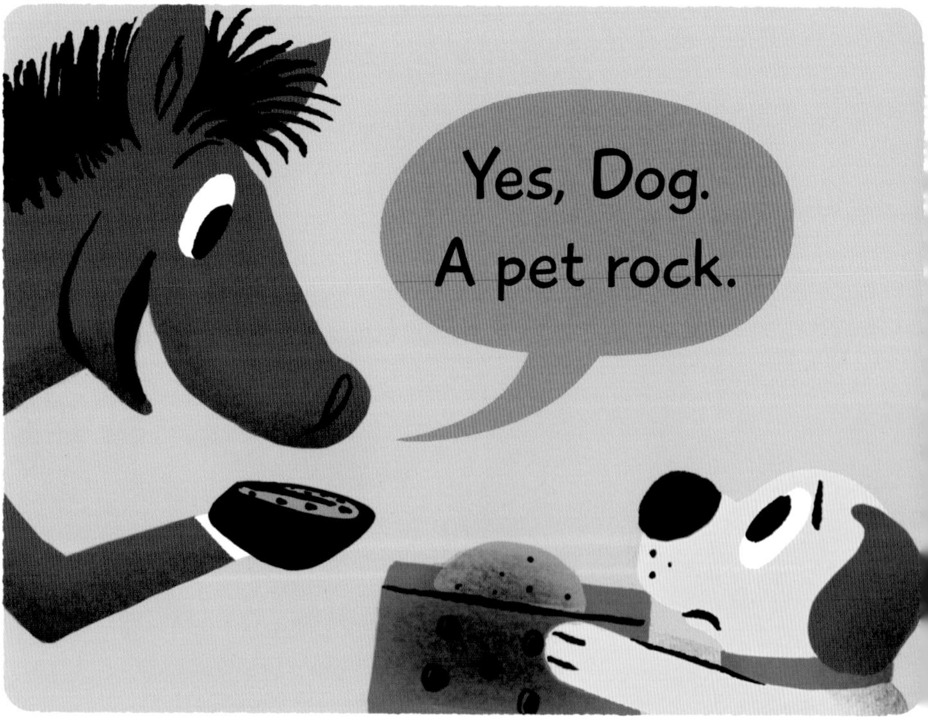
Yes, Dog.
A pet rock.

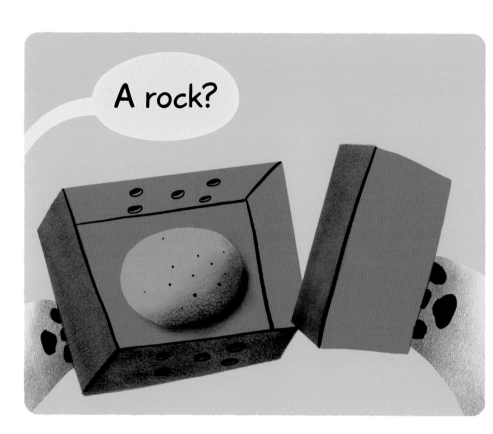

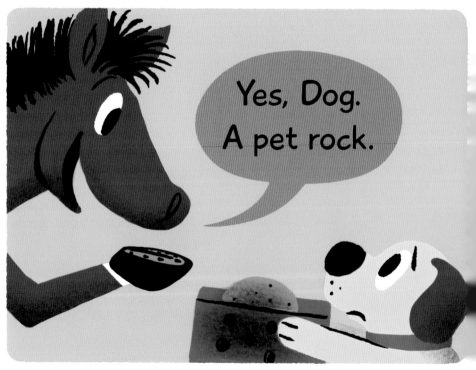

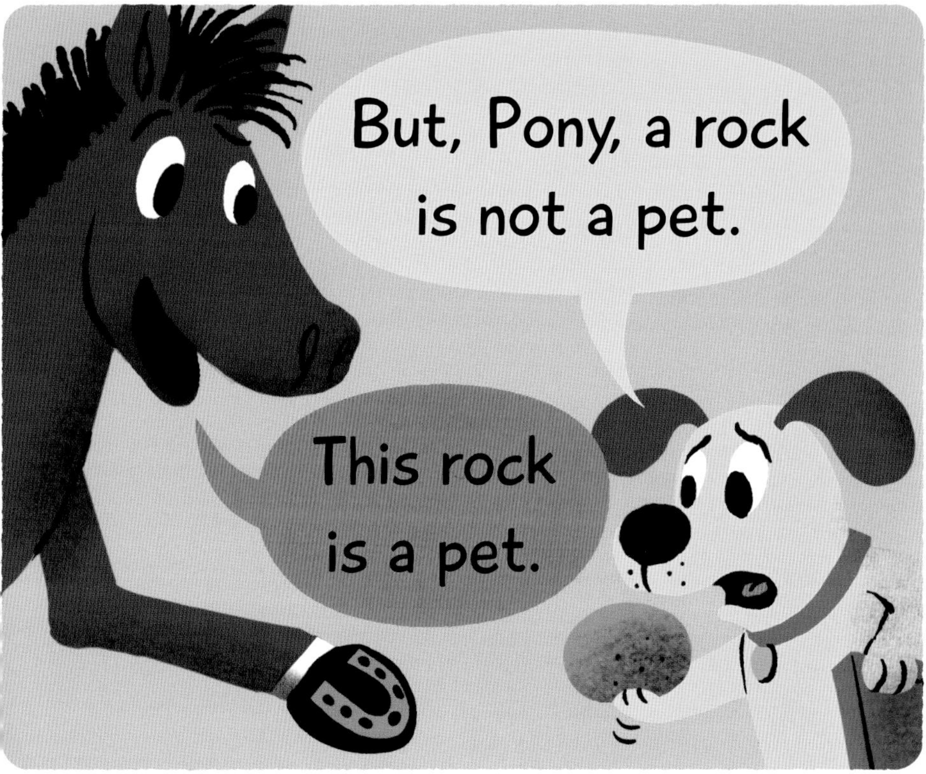
But, Pony, a rock is not a pet.
This rock is a pet.

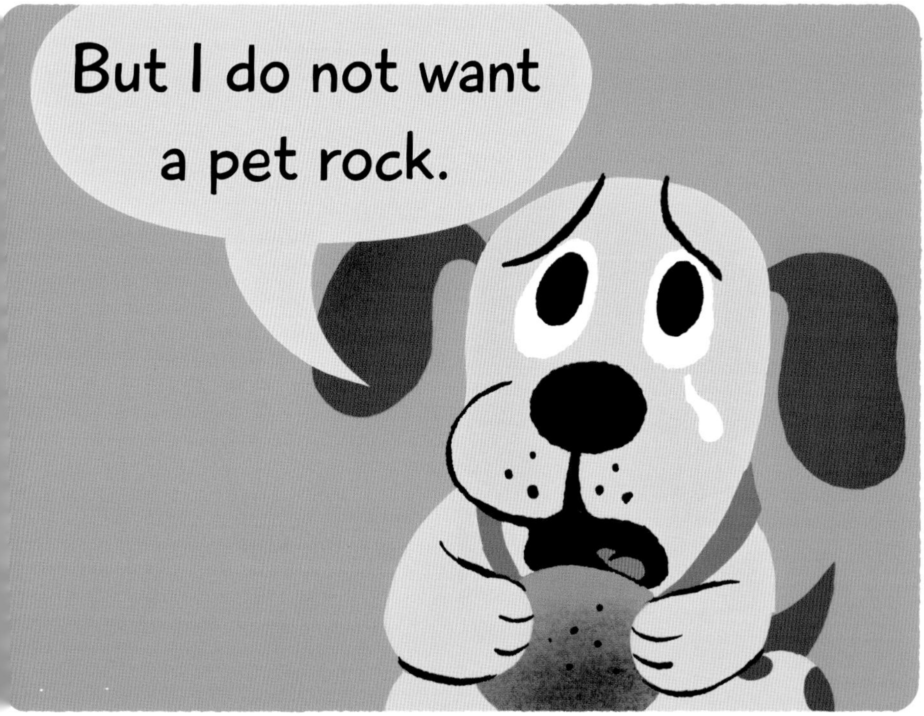
But I do not want a pet rock.

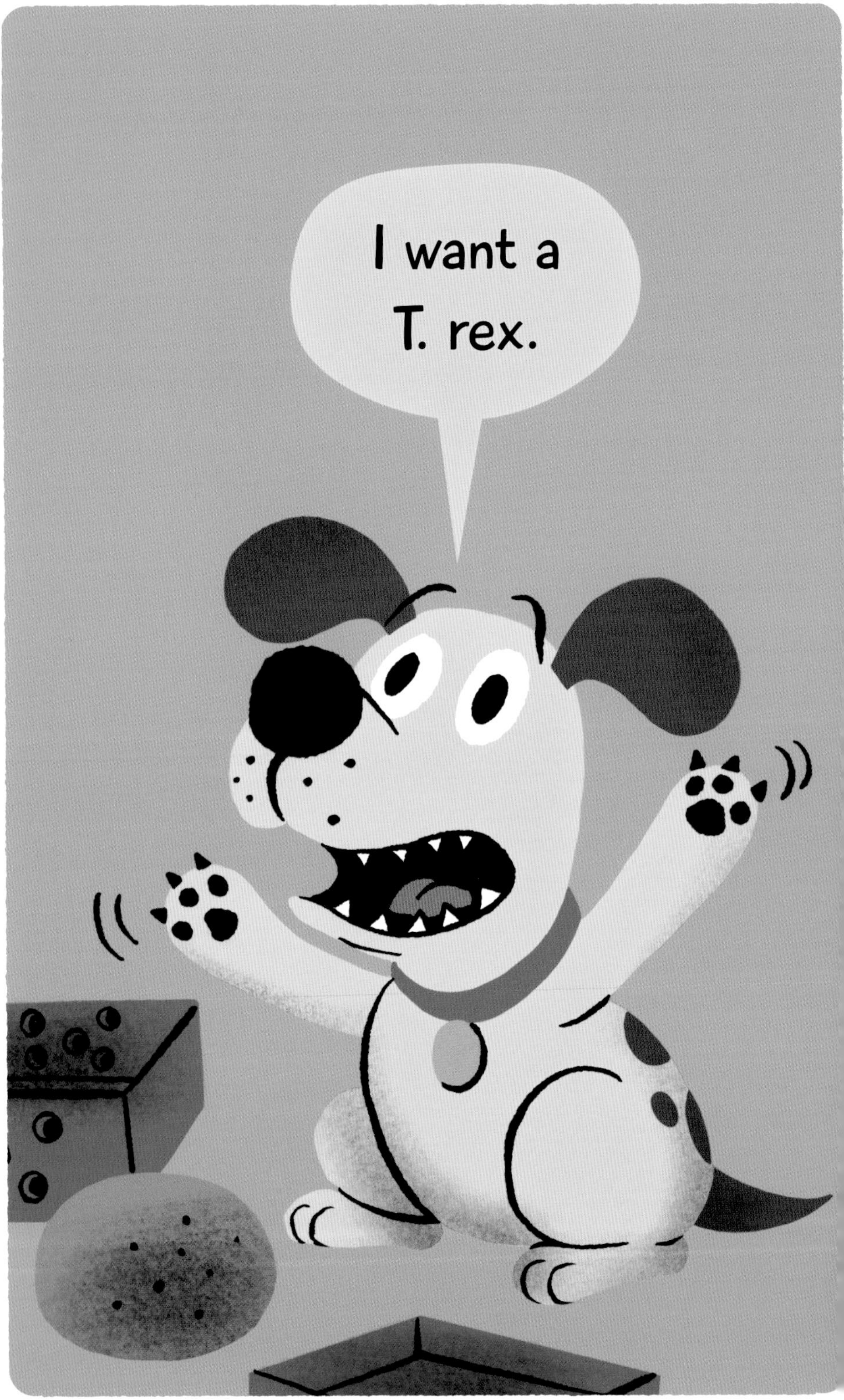
I want a T. rex.

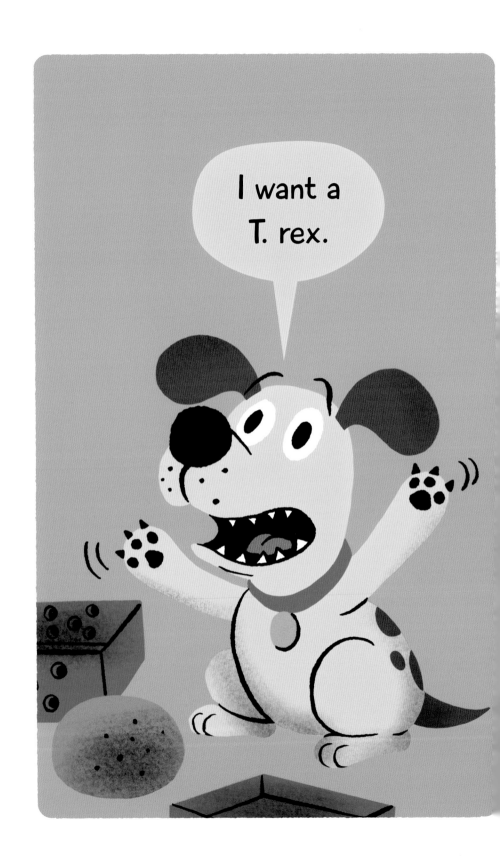

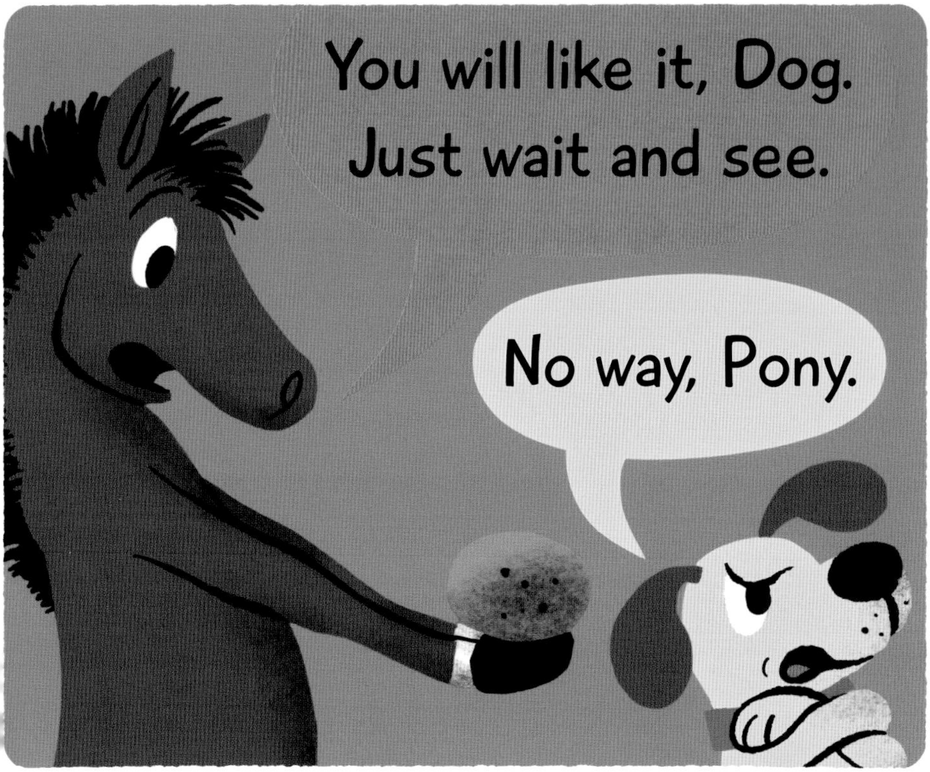
You will like it, Dog.
Just wait and see.
No way, Pony.

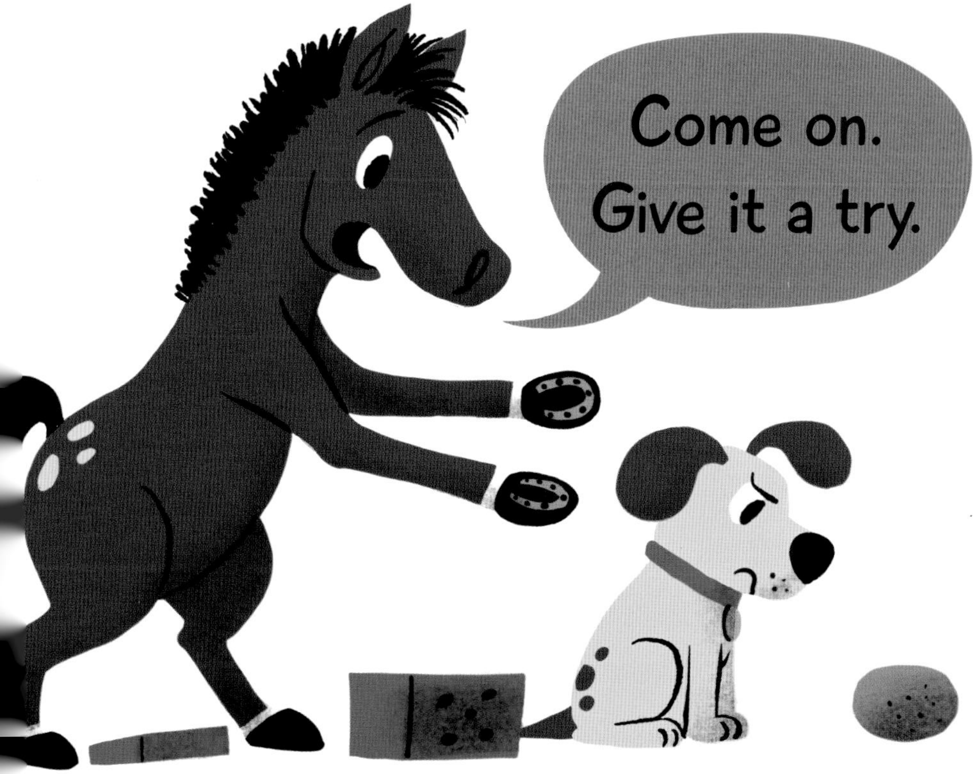
Come on.
Give it a try.

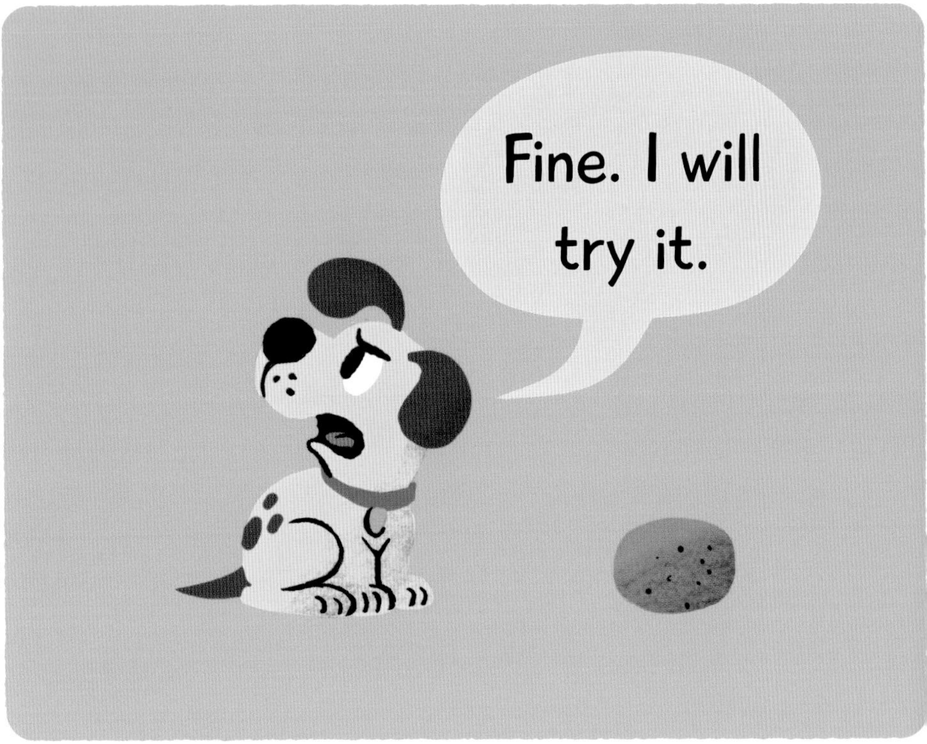
Fine. I will try it.

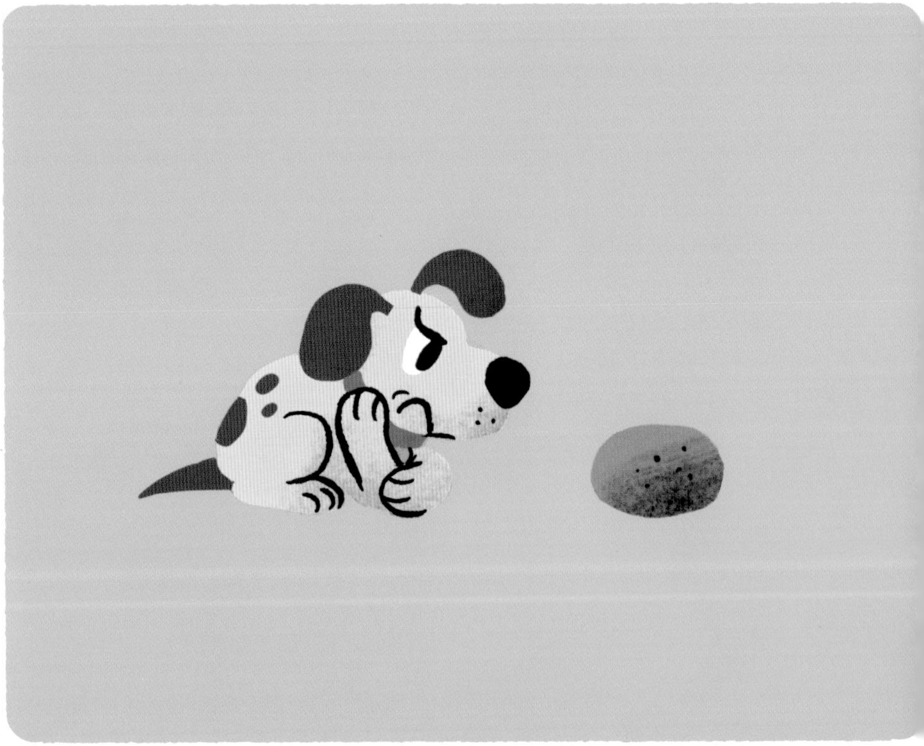

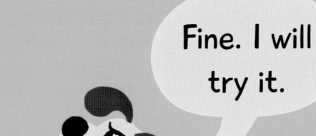

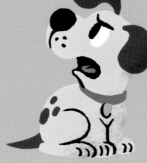

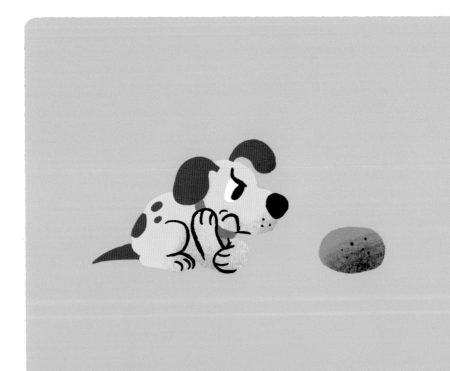

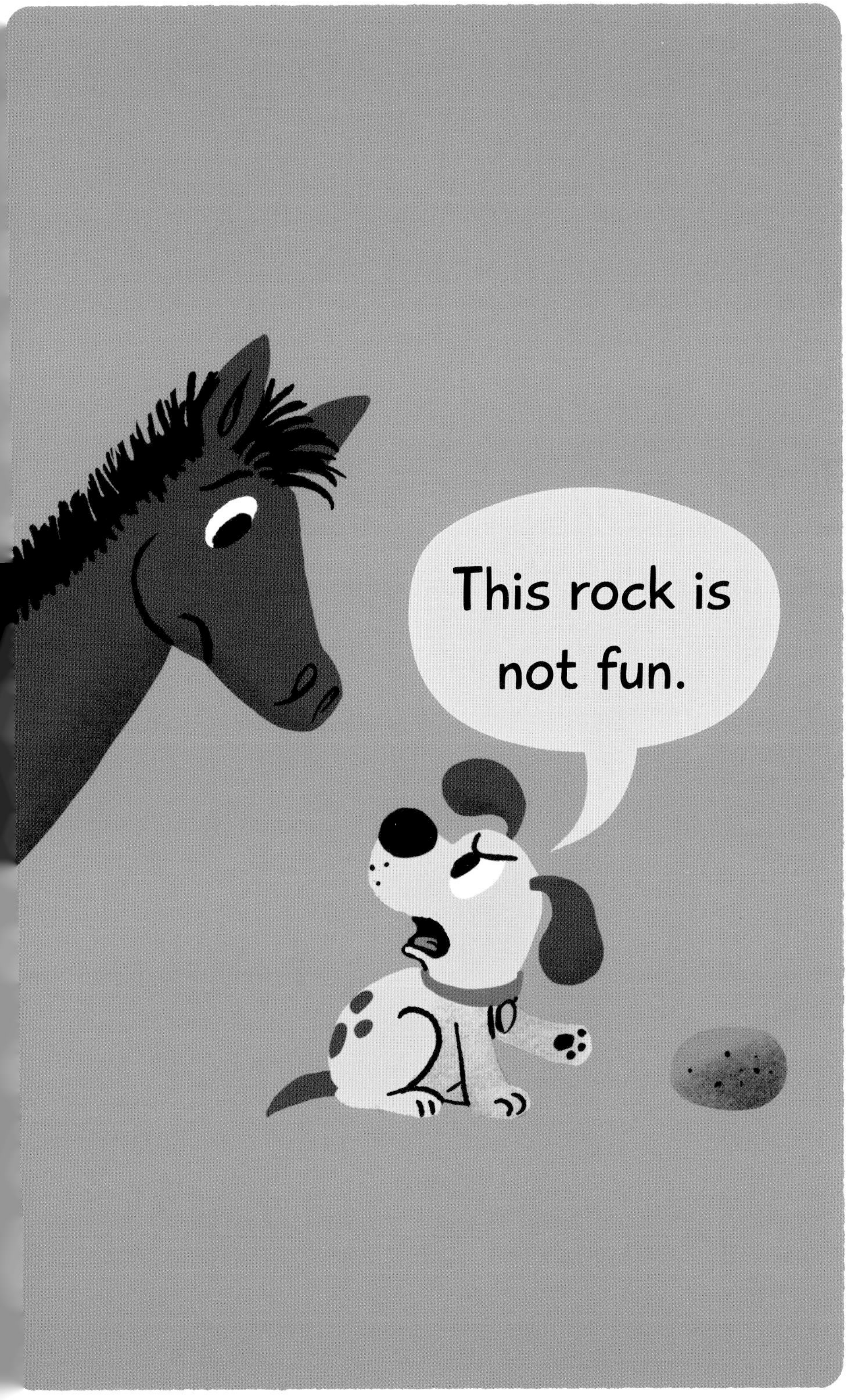
This rock is not fun.

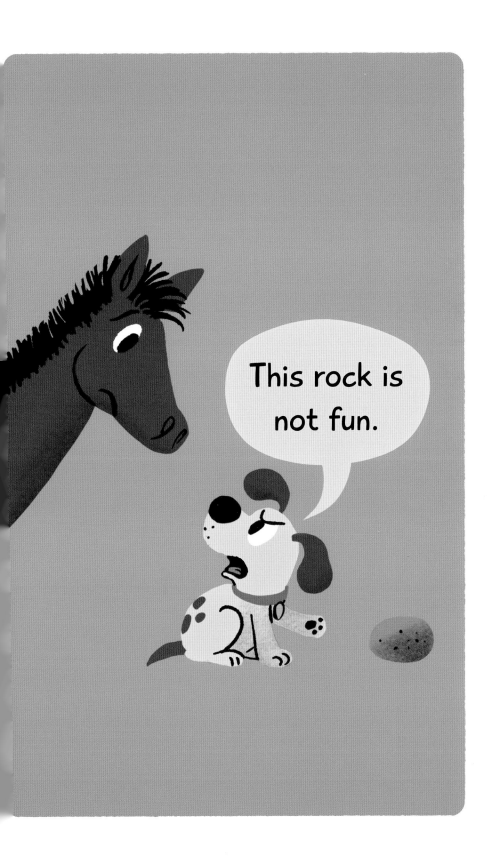

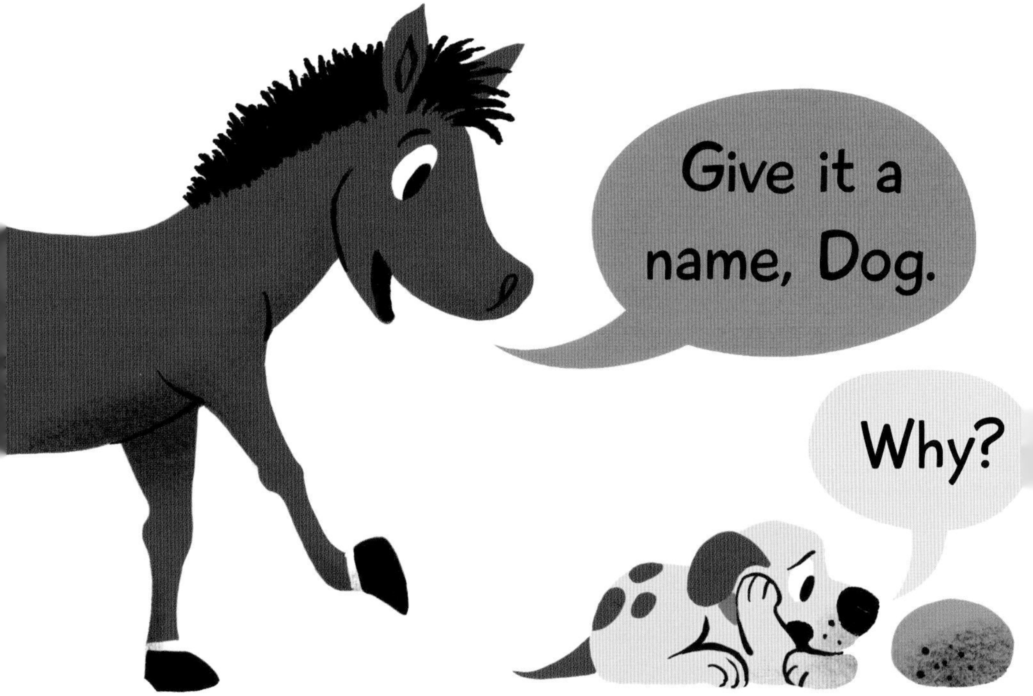
Give it a name, Dog.
Why?

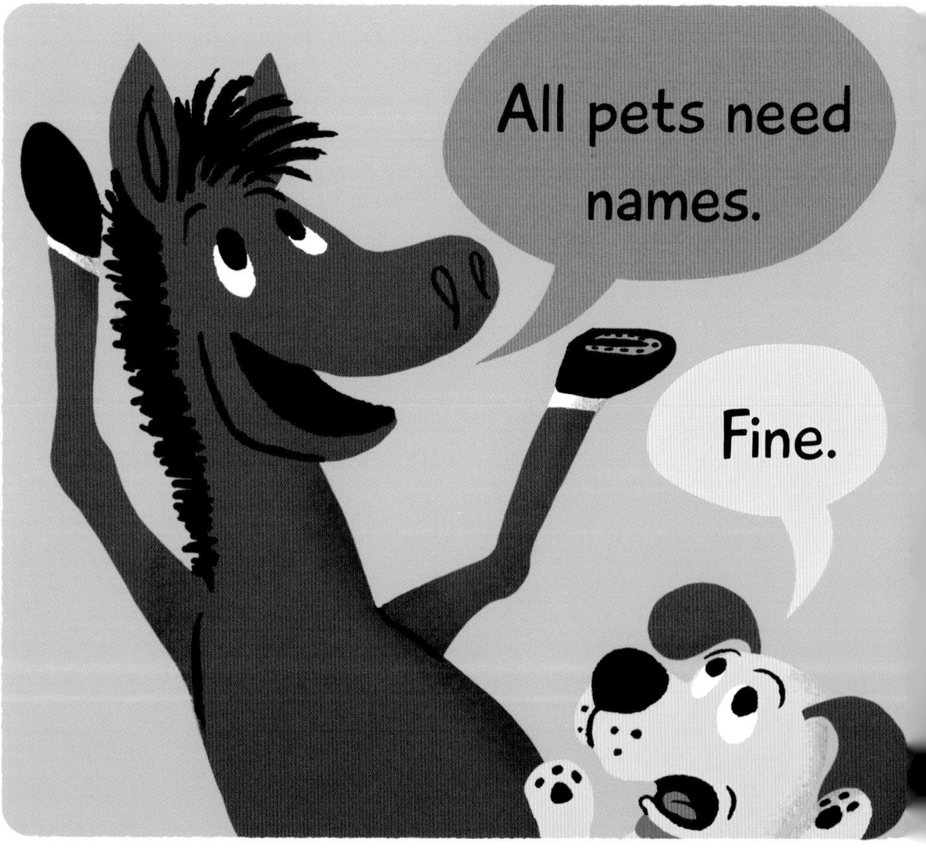
All pets need names.
Fine.

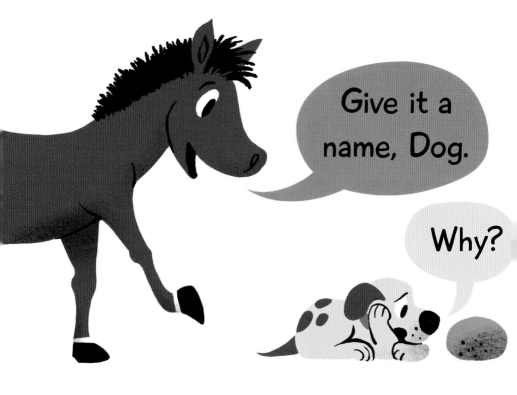

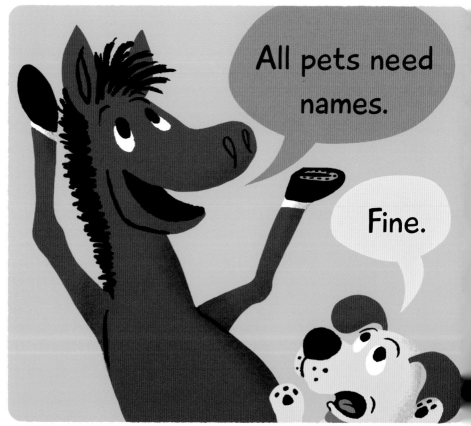

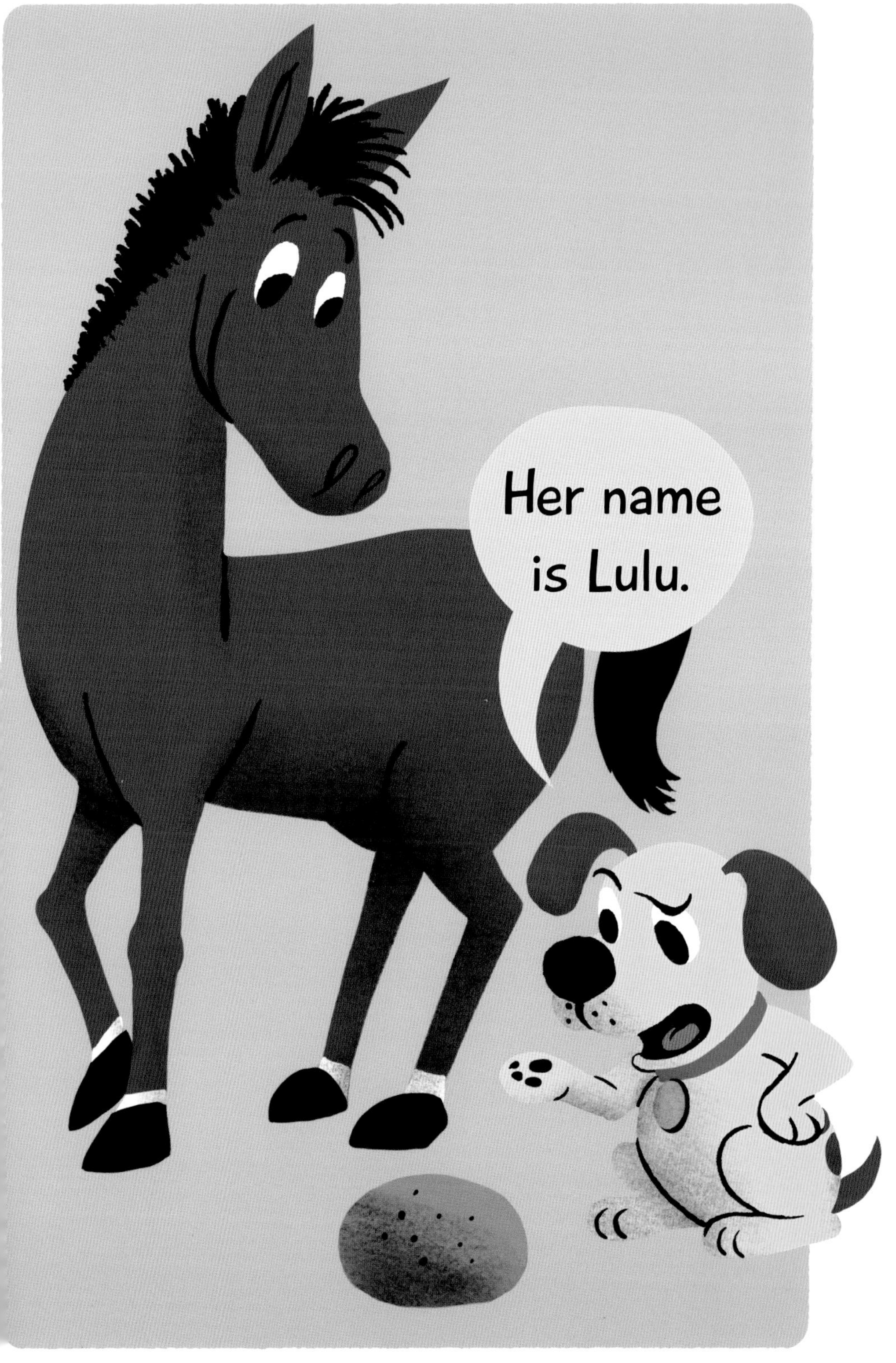
Her name
is Lulu.

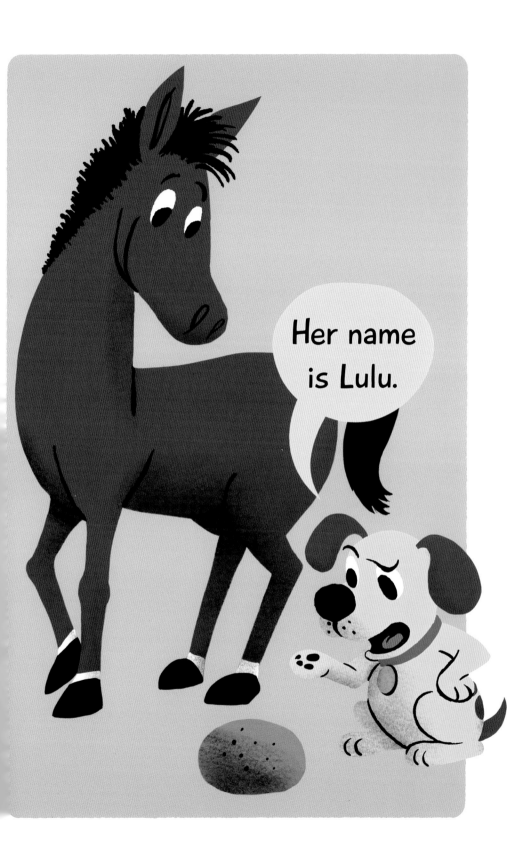

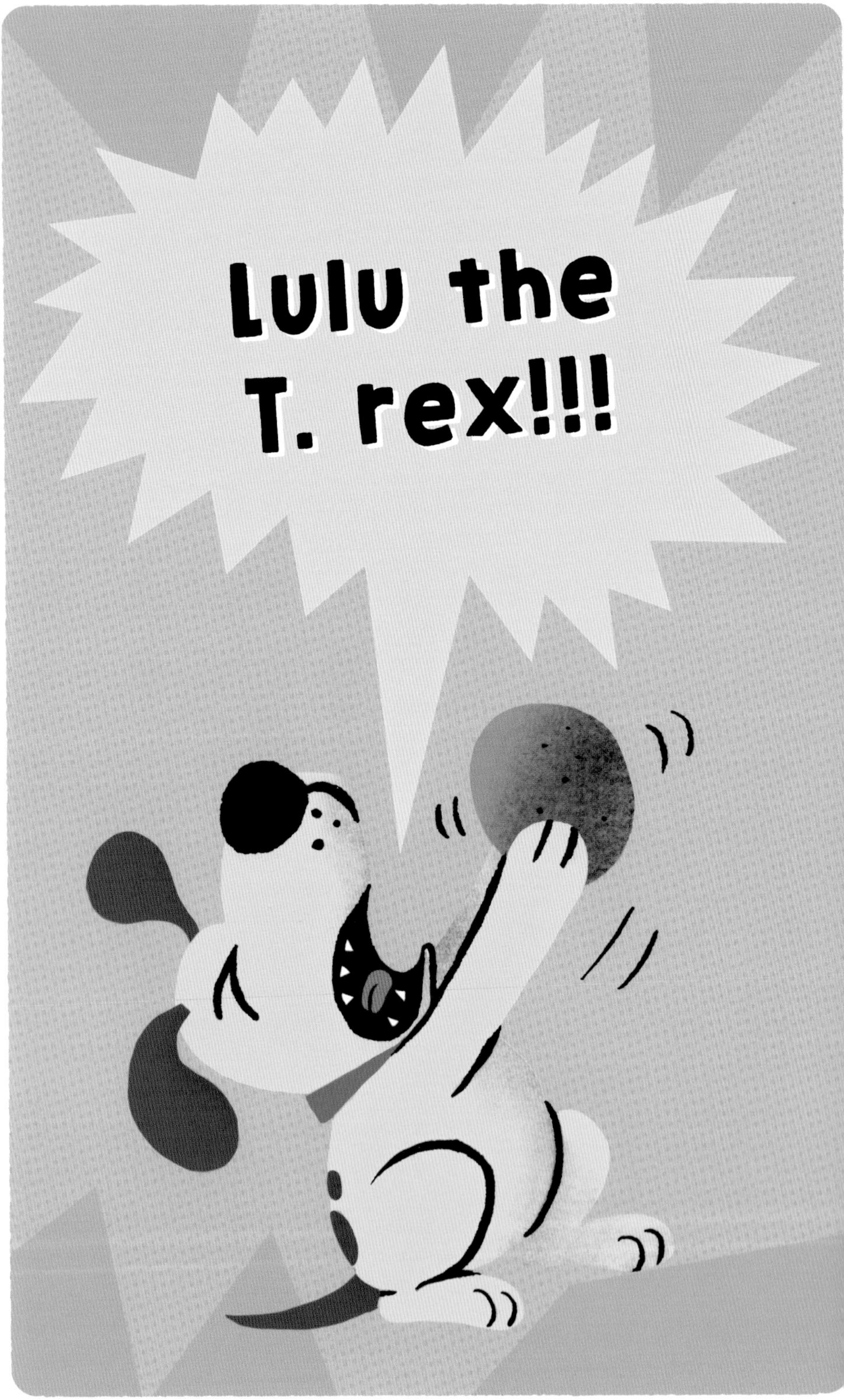
Lulu the
T. rex!!!

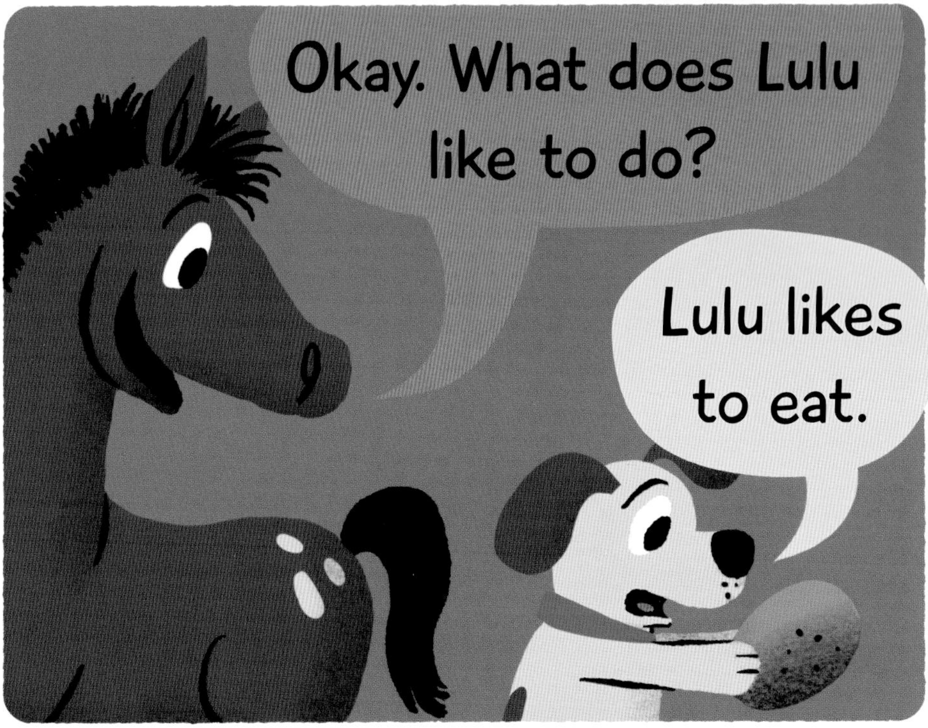
Okay. What does Lulu like to do?
Lulu likes to eat.

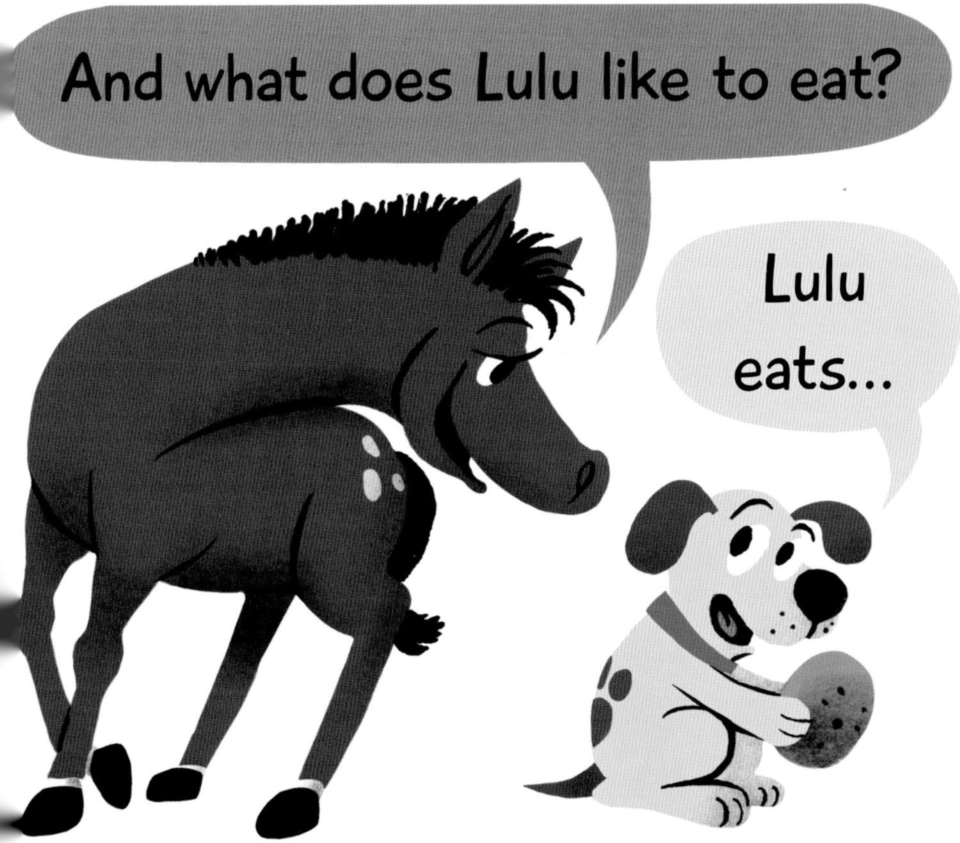
And what does Lulu like to eat?
Lulu
Lulu eats...

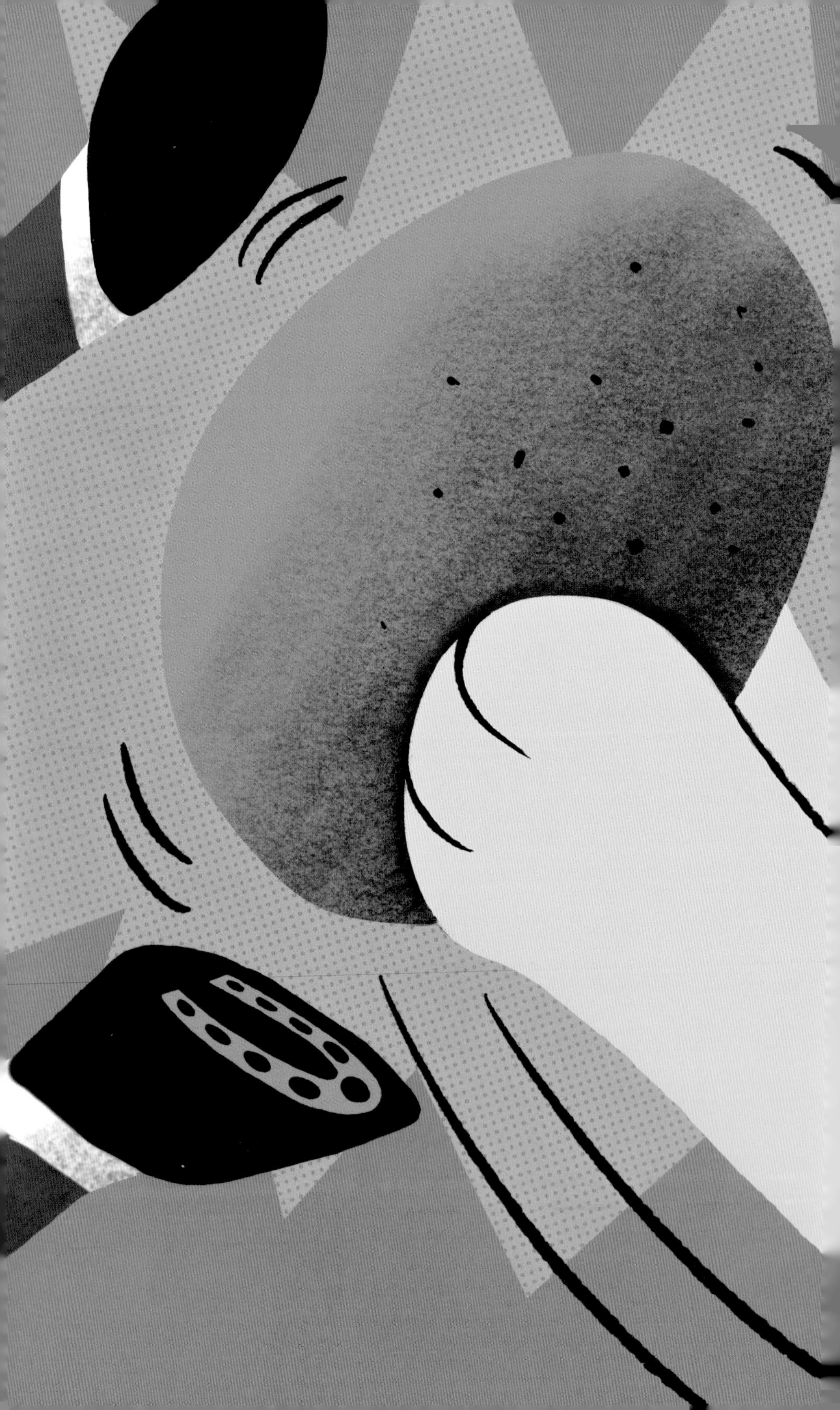

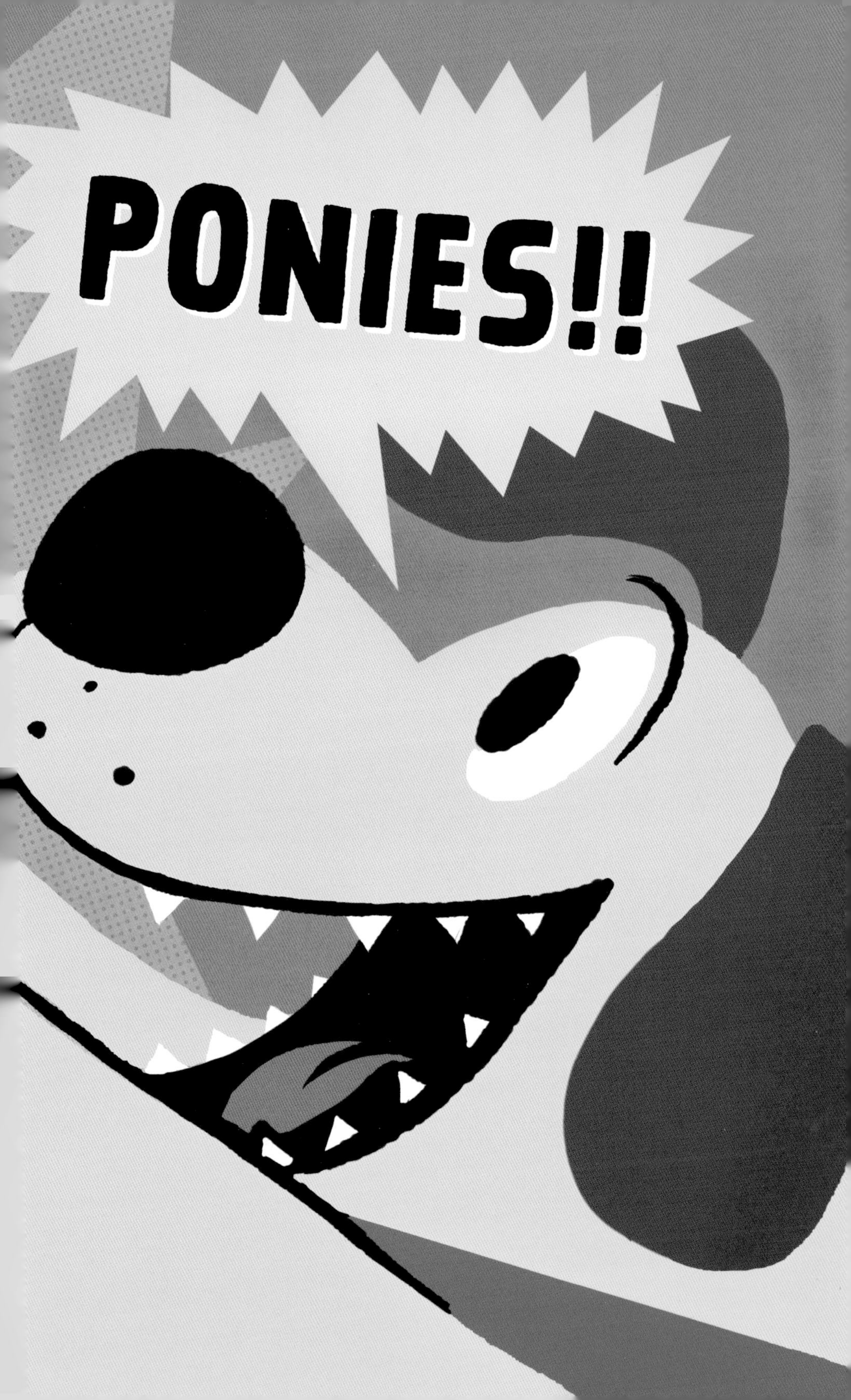
PONIES!!

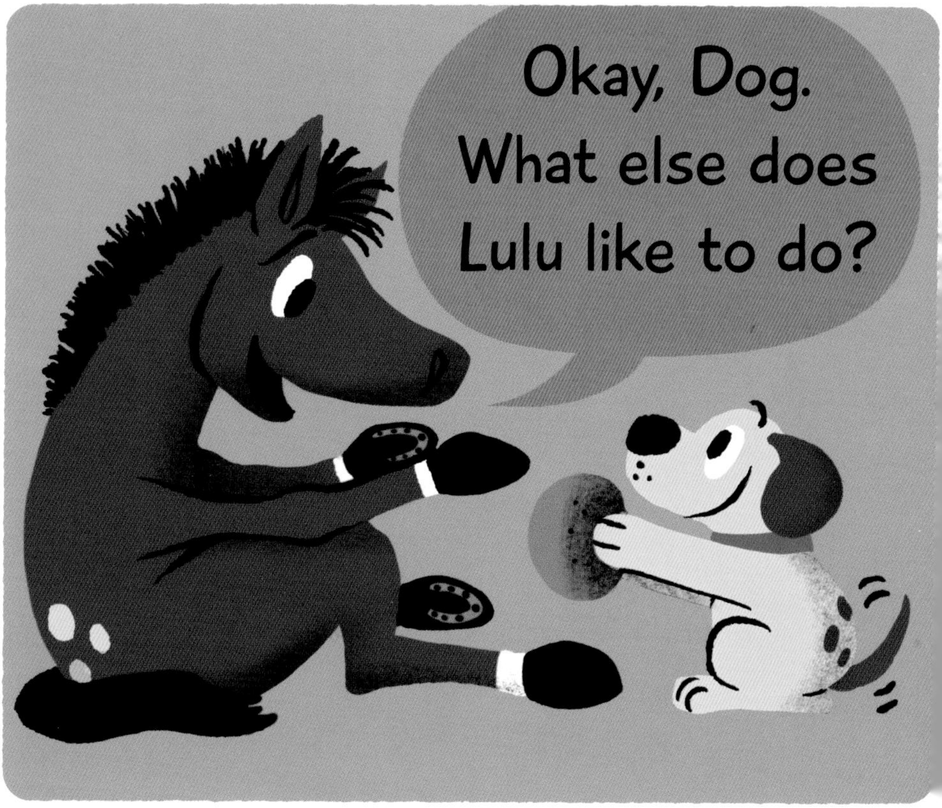
Okay, Dog.
What else does
Lulu like to do?

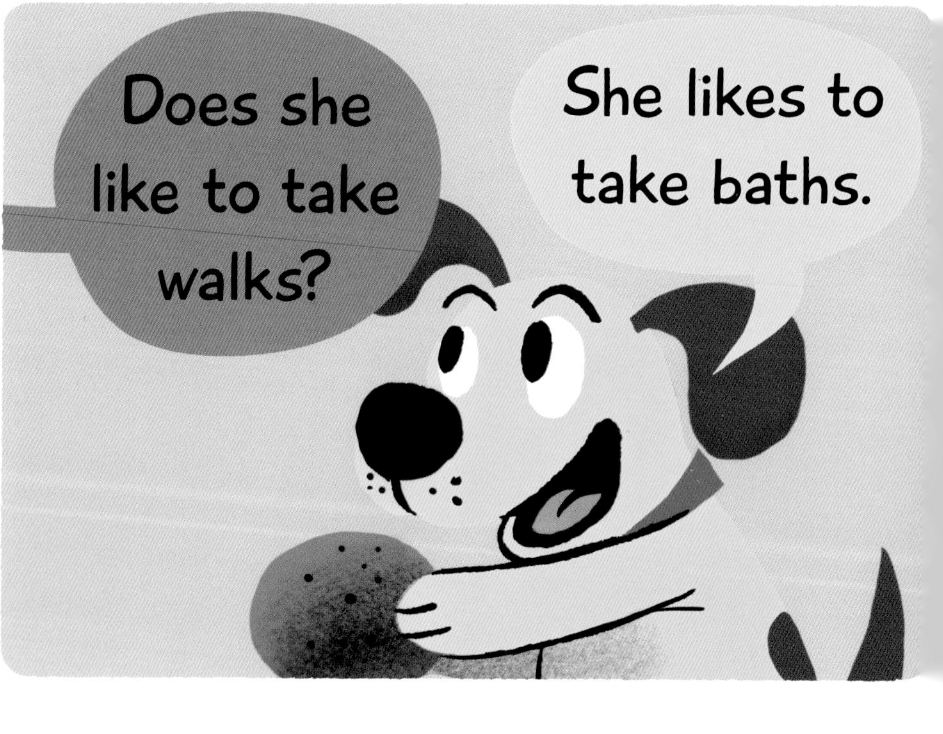
Does she
like to take
walks?
She likes to
take baths.

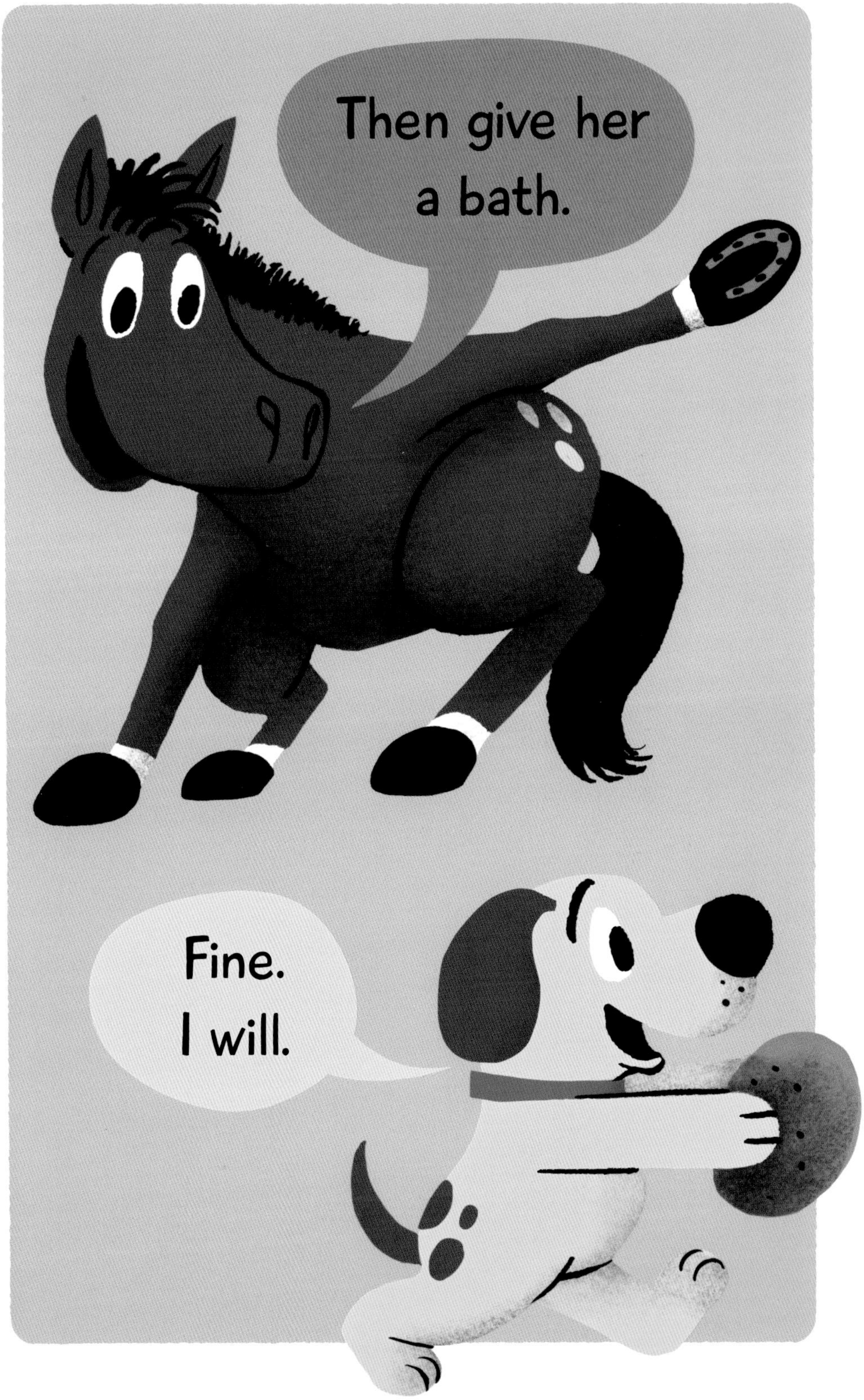
Then give her a bath.
Fine. I will.

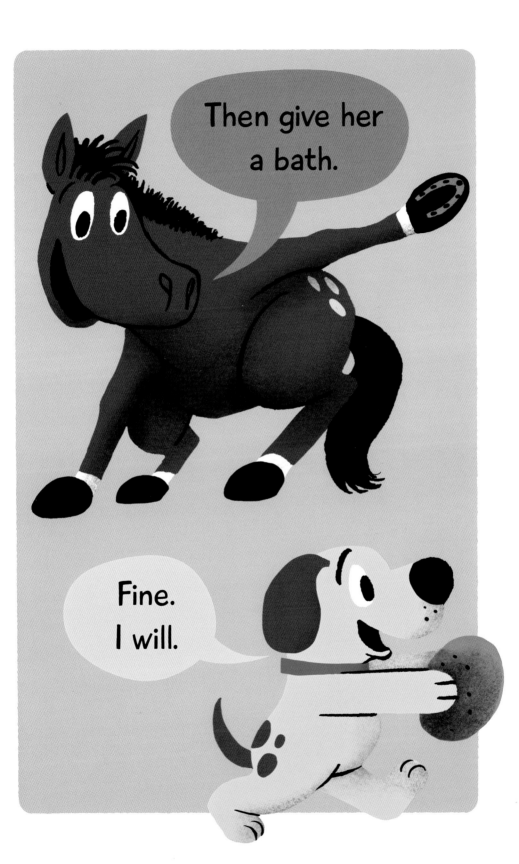

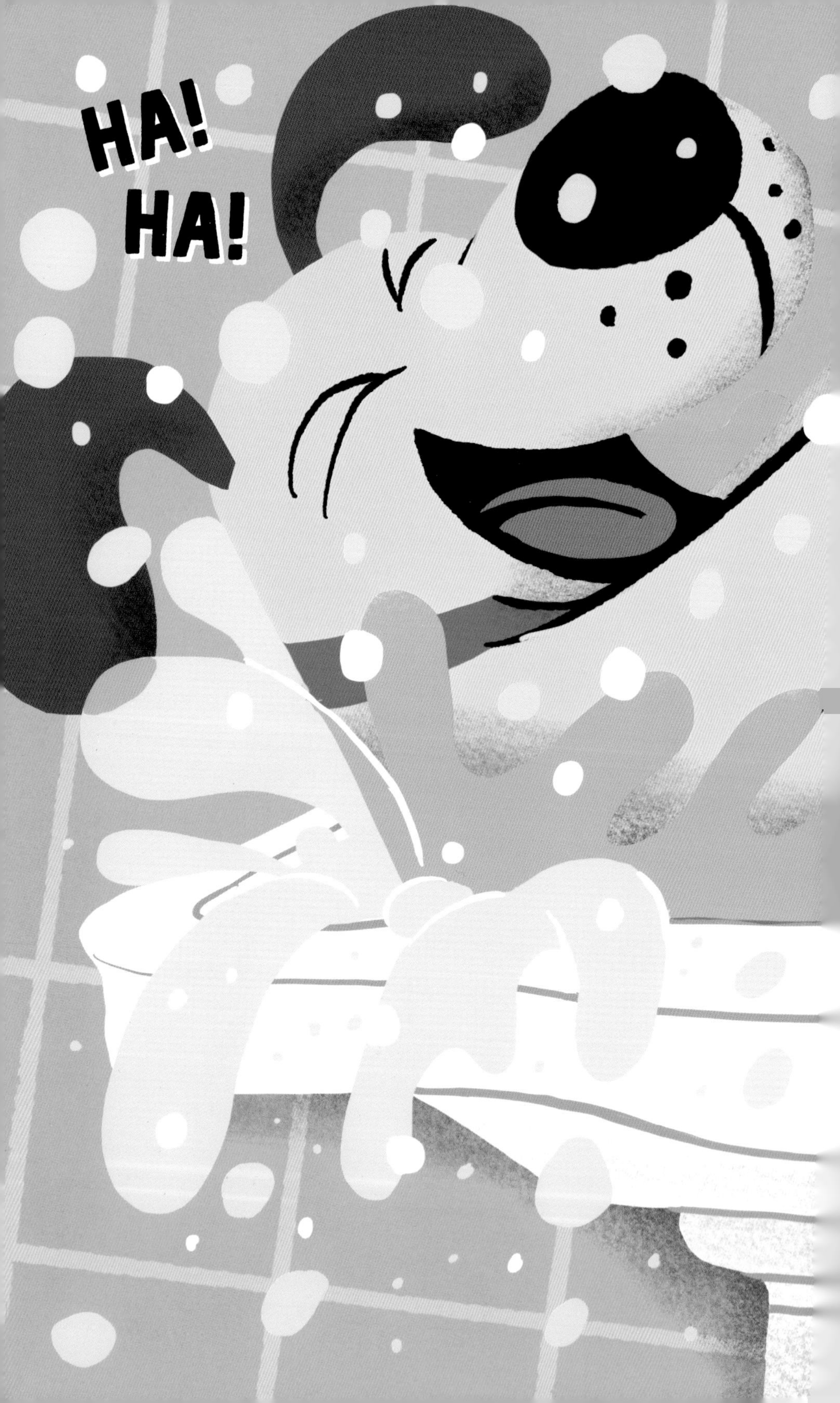
HA!
HA!

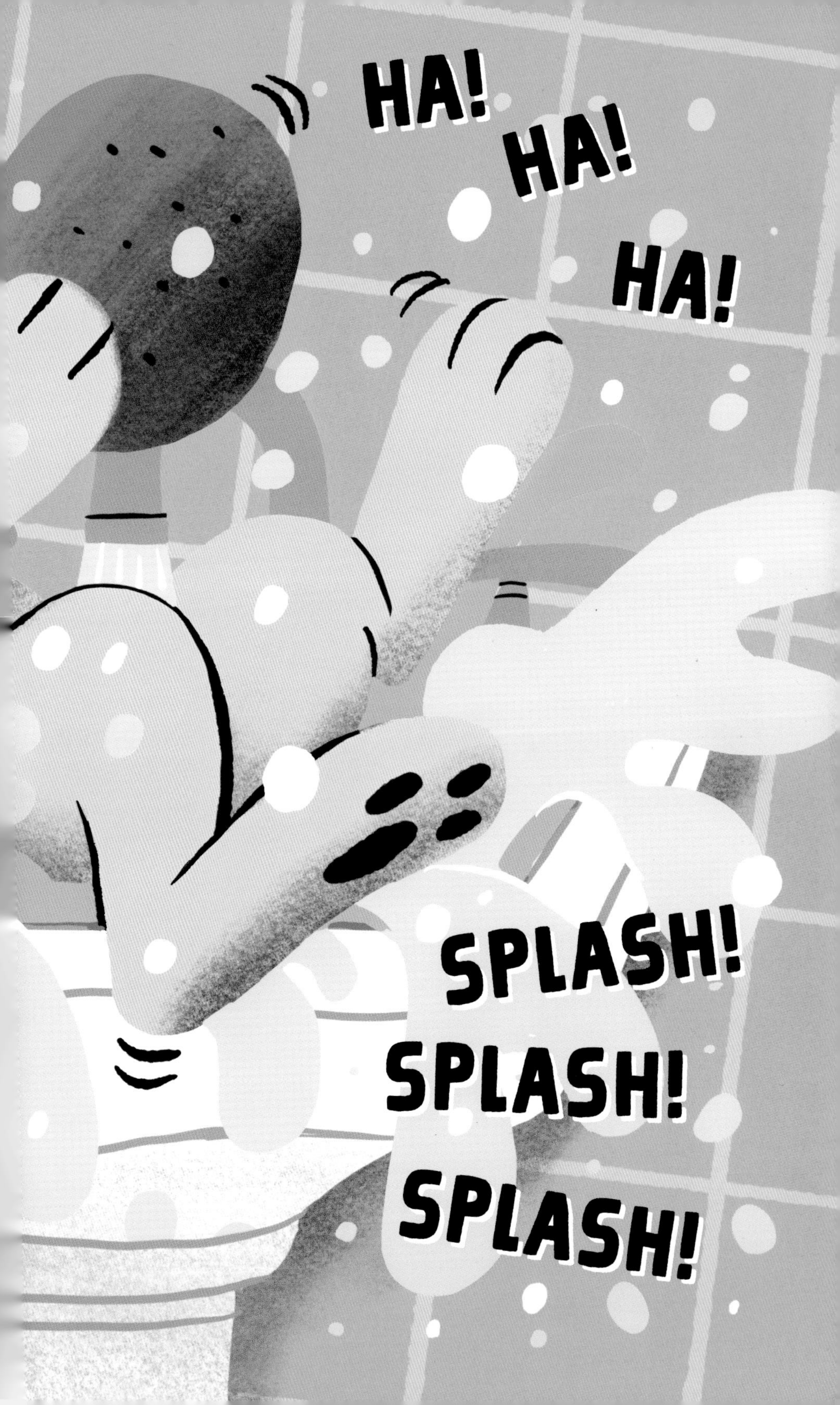
HA!
HA!
HA!
SPLASH!
SPLASH!
SPLASH!

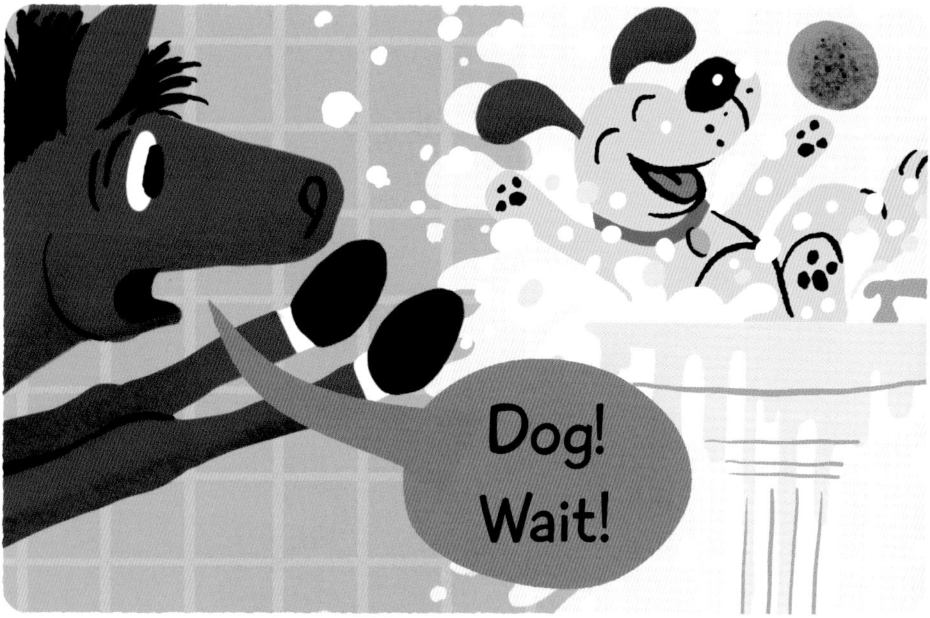
Dog!
Wait!

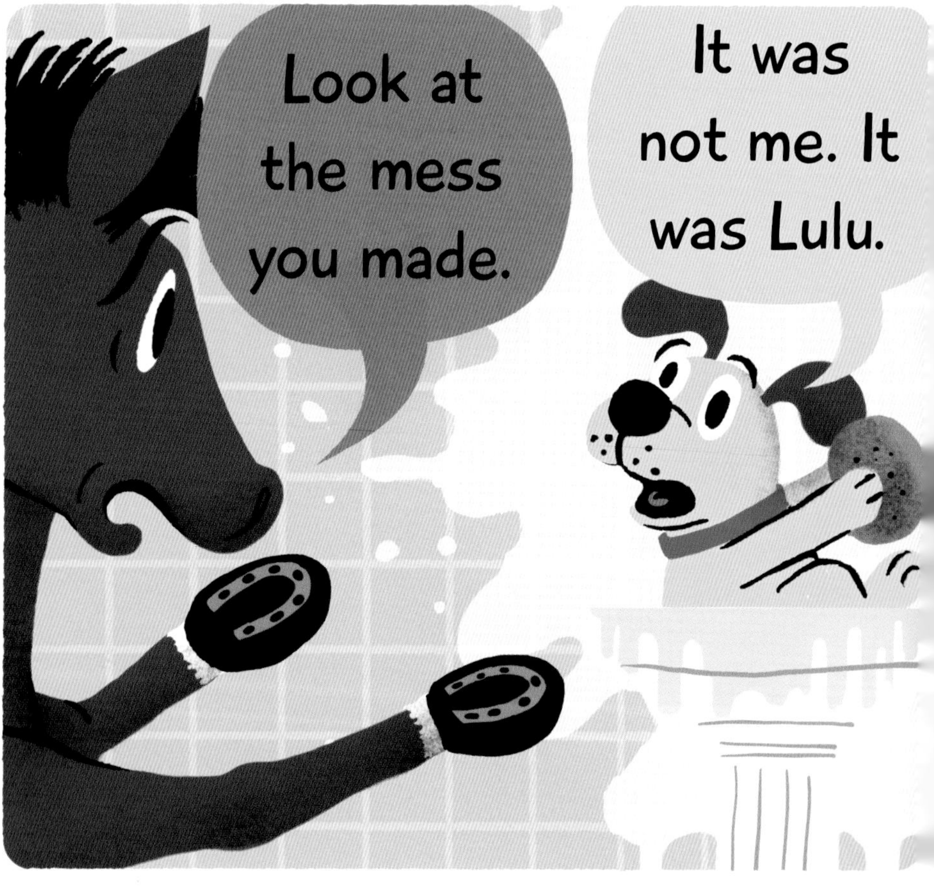
Look at the mess you made.
It was not me. It was Lulu.

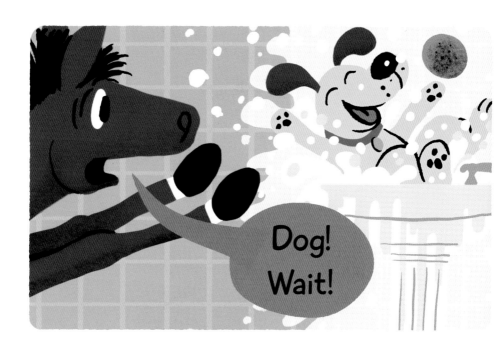

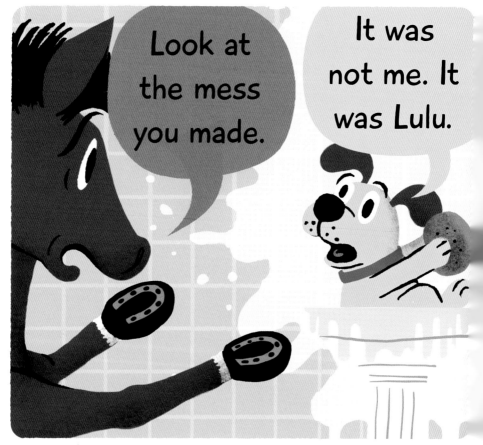

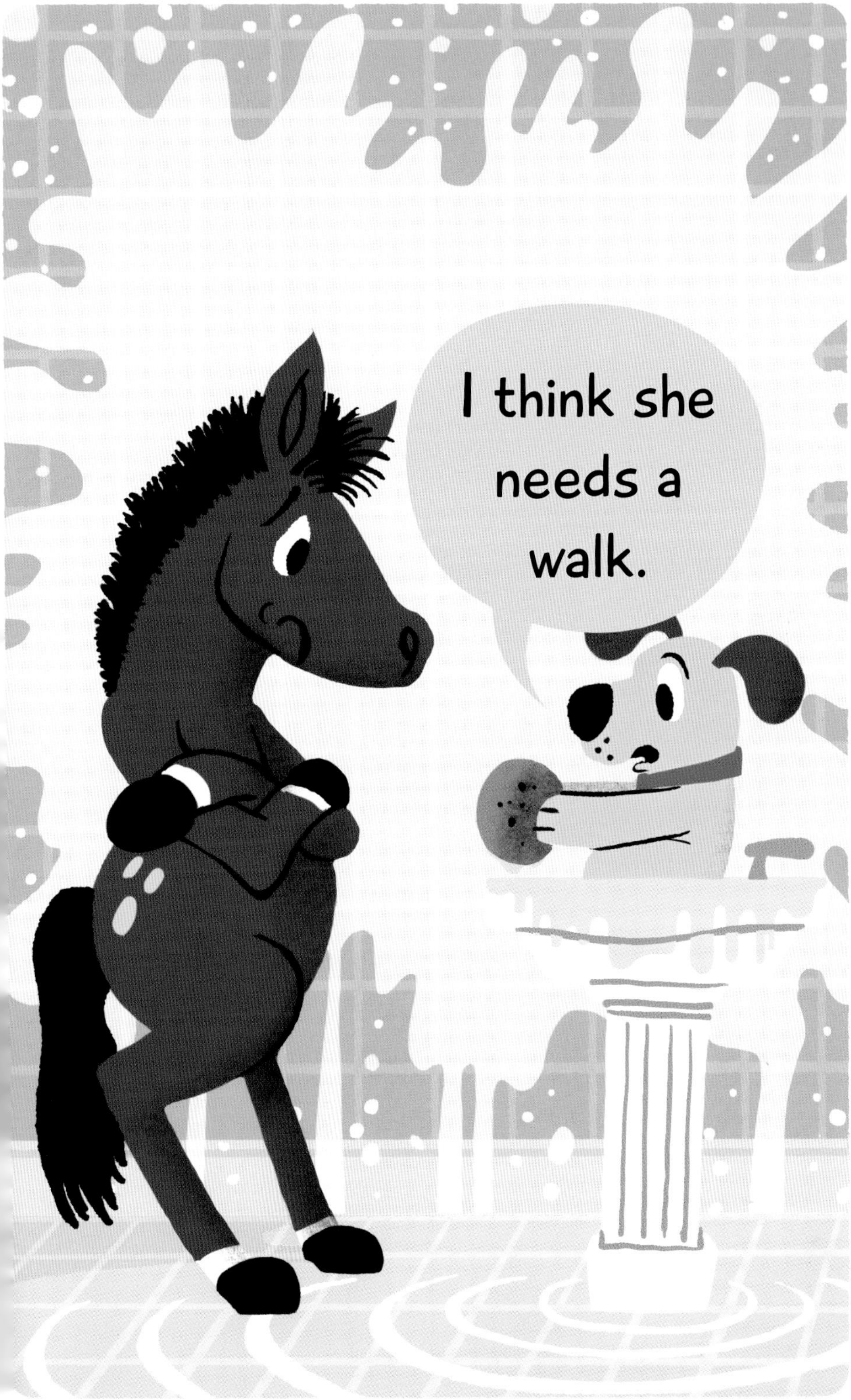
I think she needs a walk.

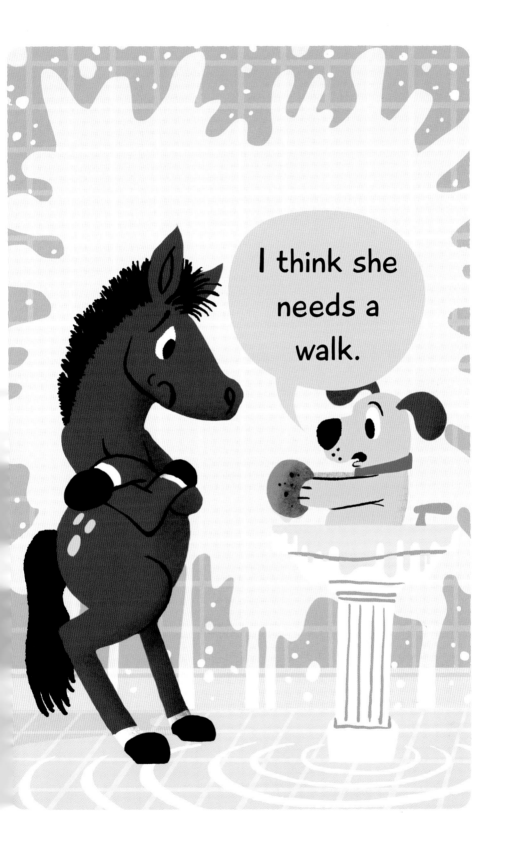

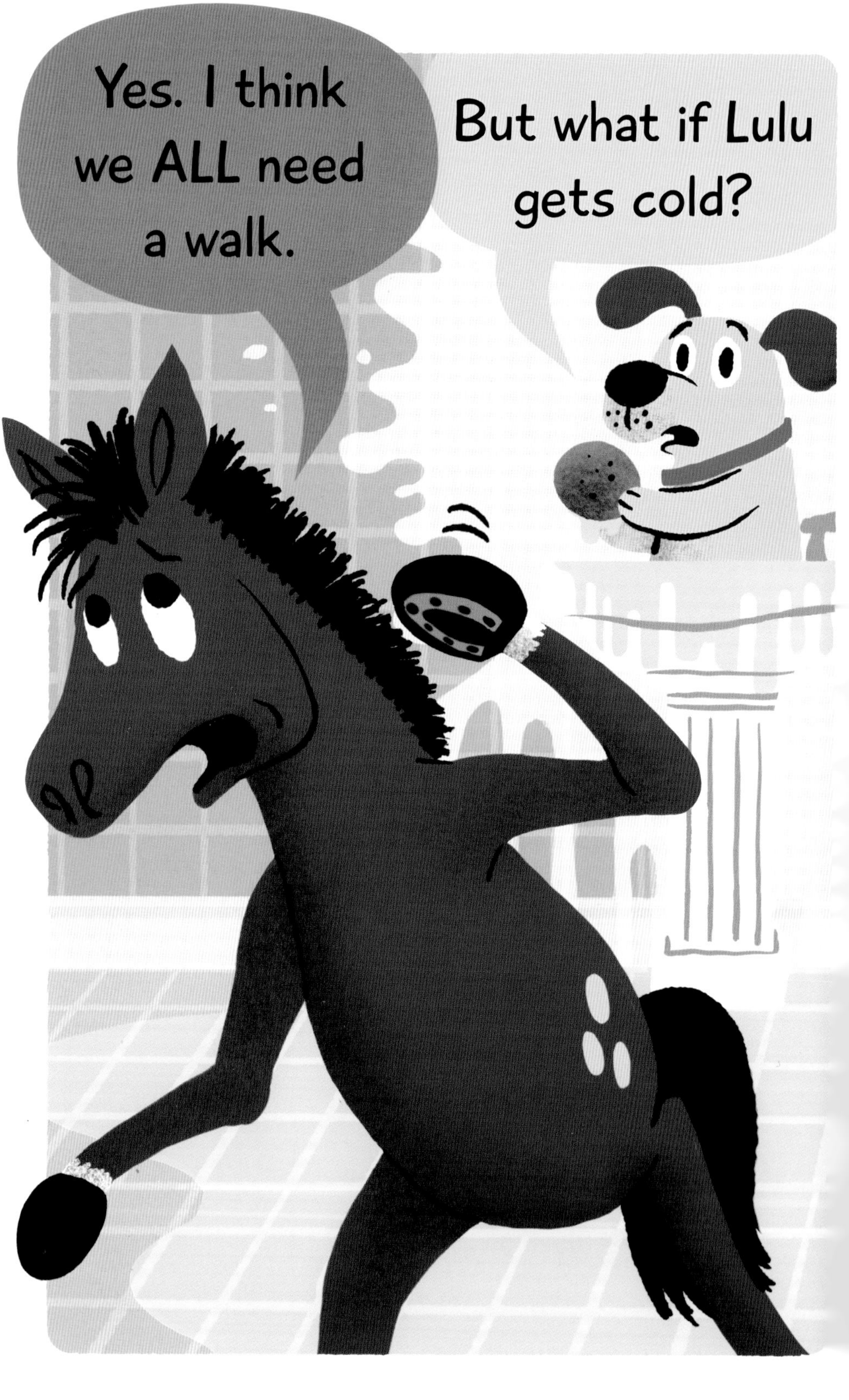
Yes. I think we ALL need a walk.
But what if Lulu gets cold?

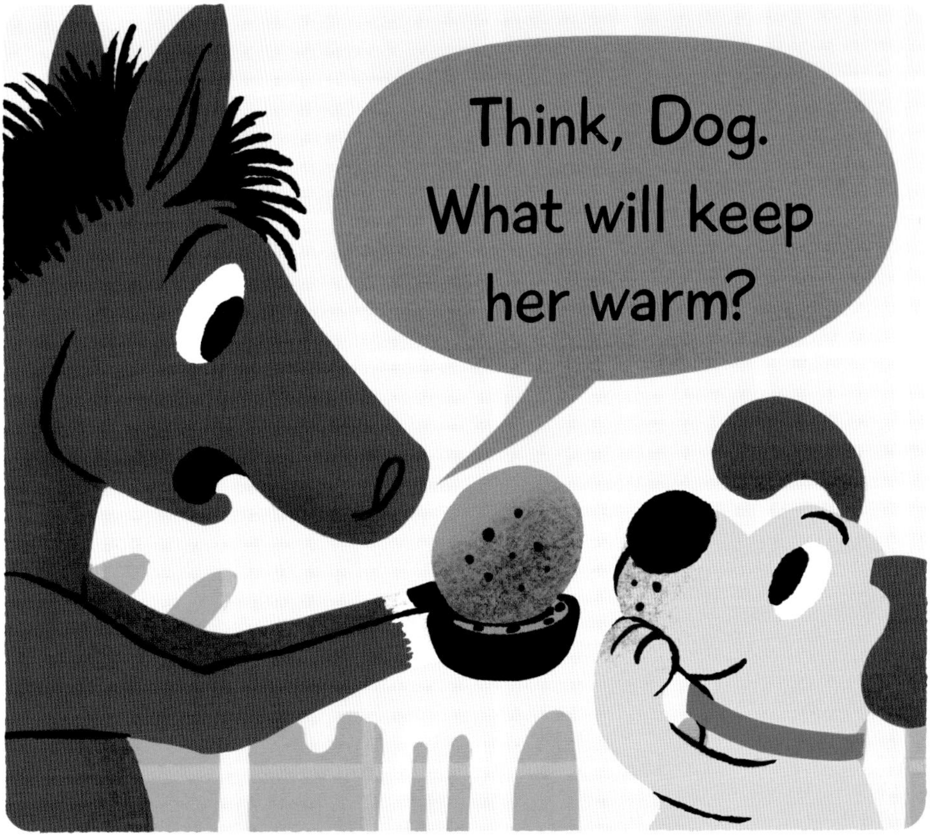
Think, Dog.
What will keep
her warm?

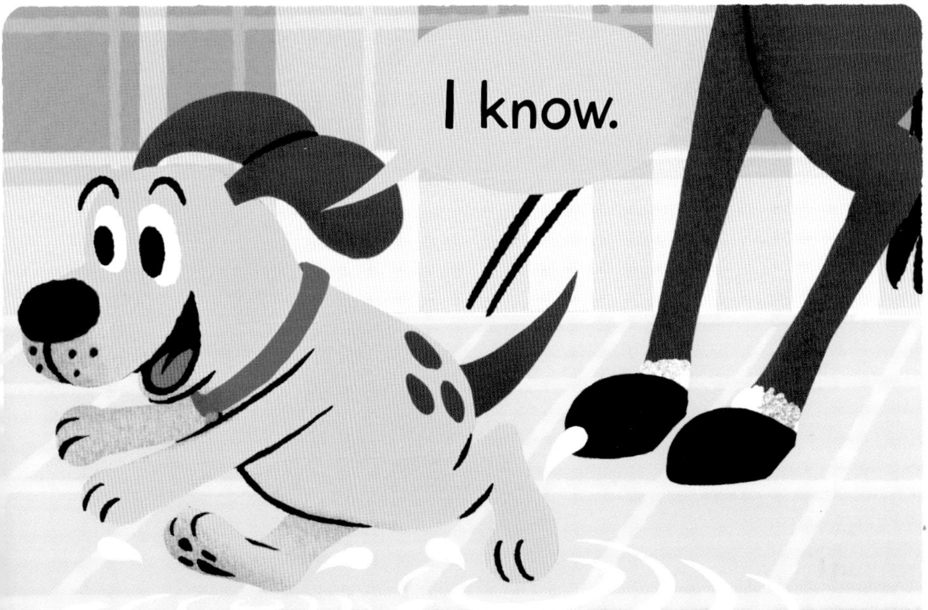
I know.

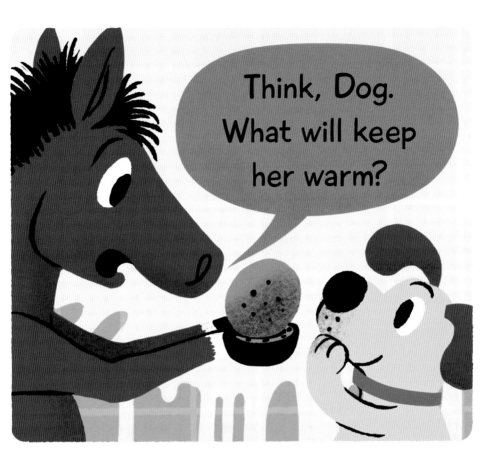

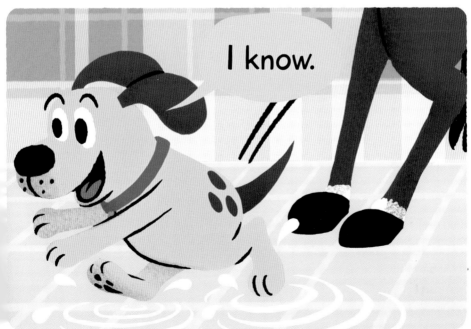

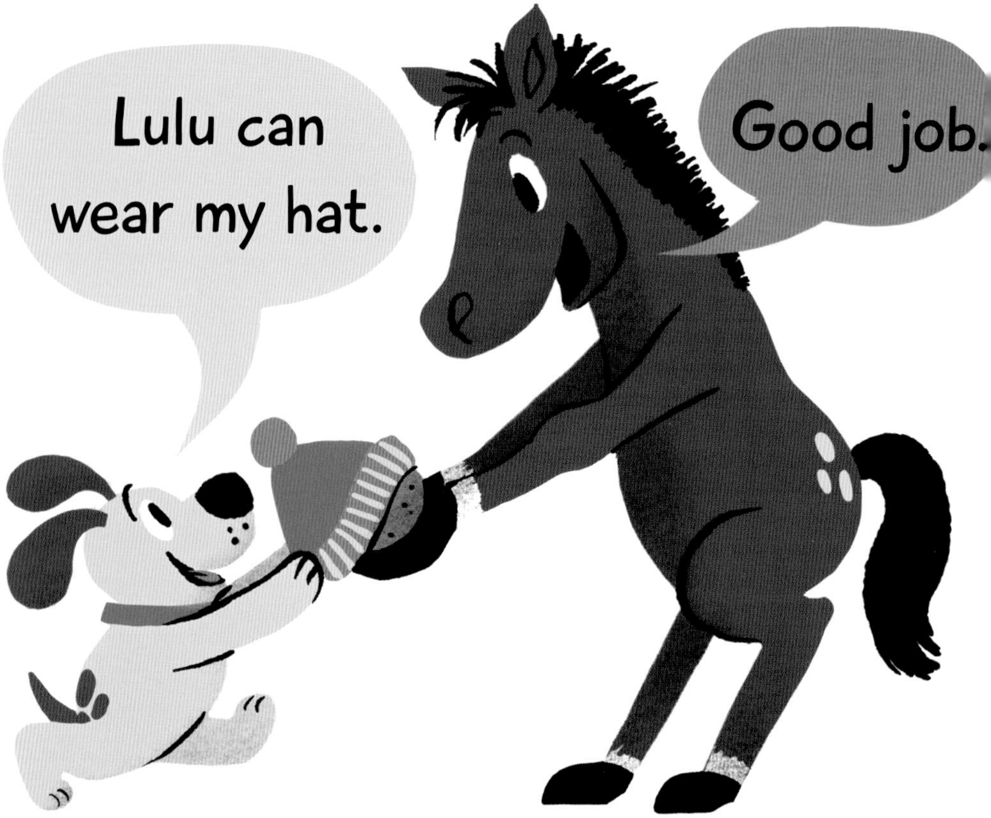
Lulu can wear my hat.
Good job.

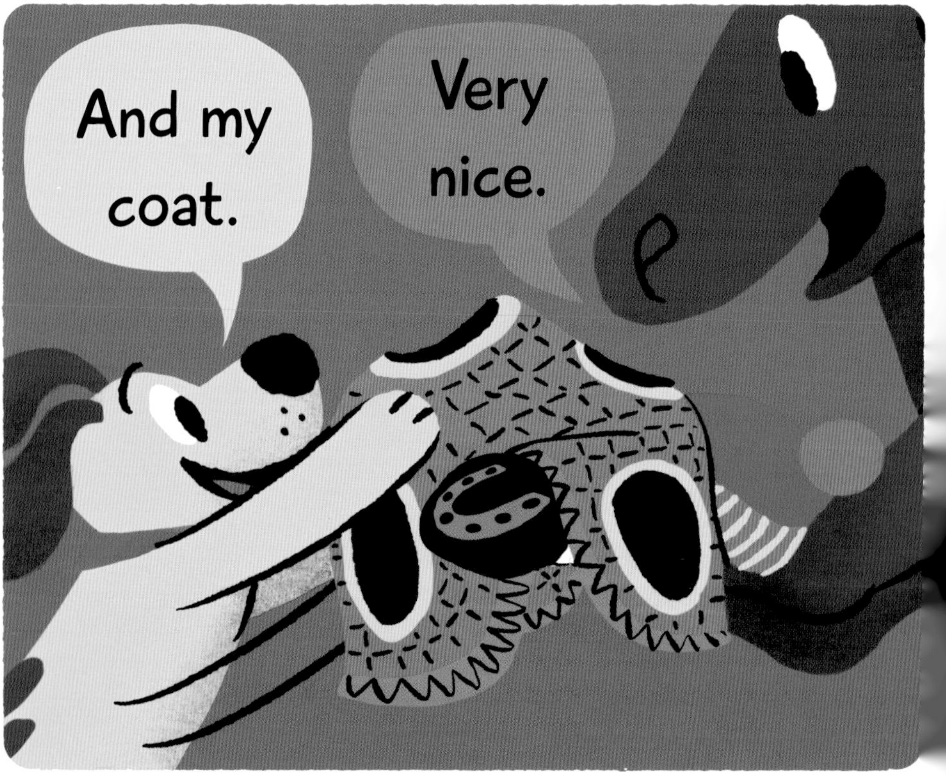
And my coat.
Very nice.

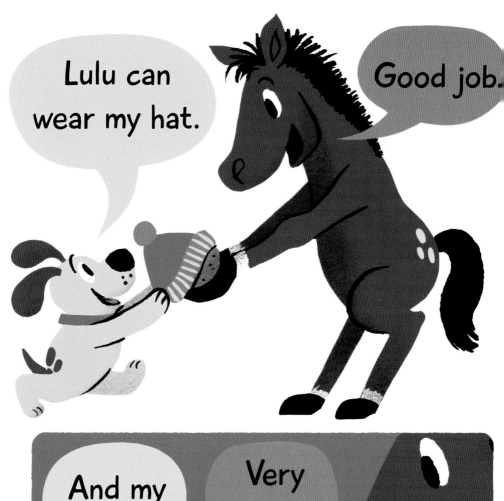

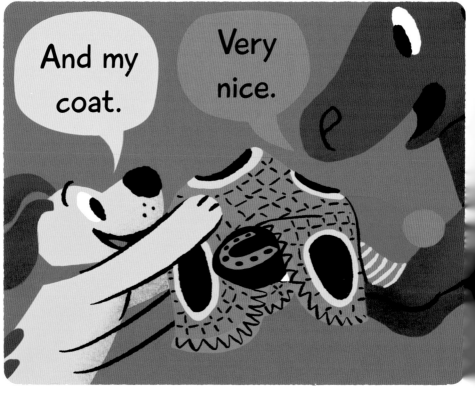

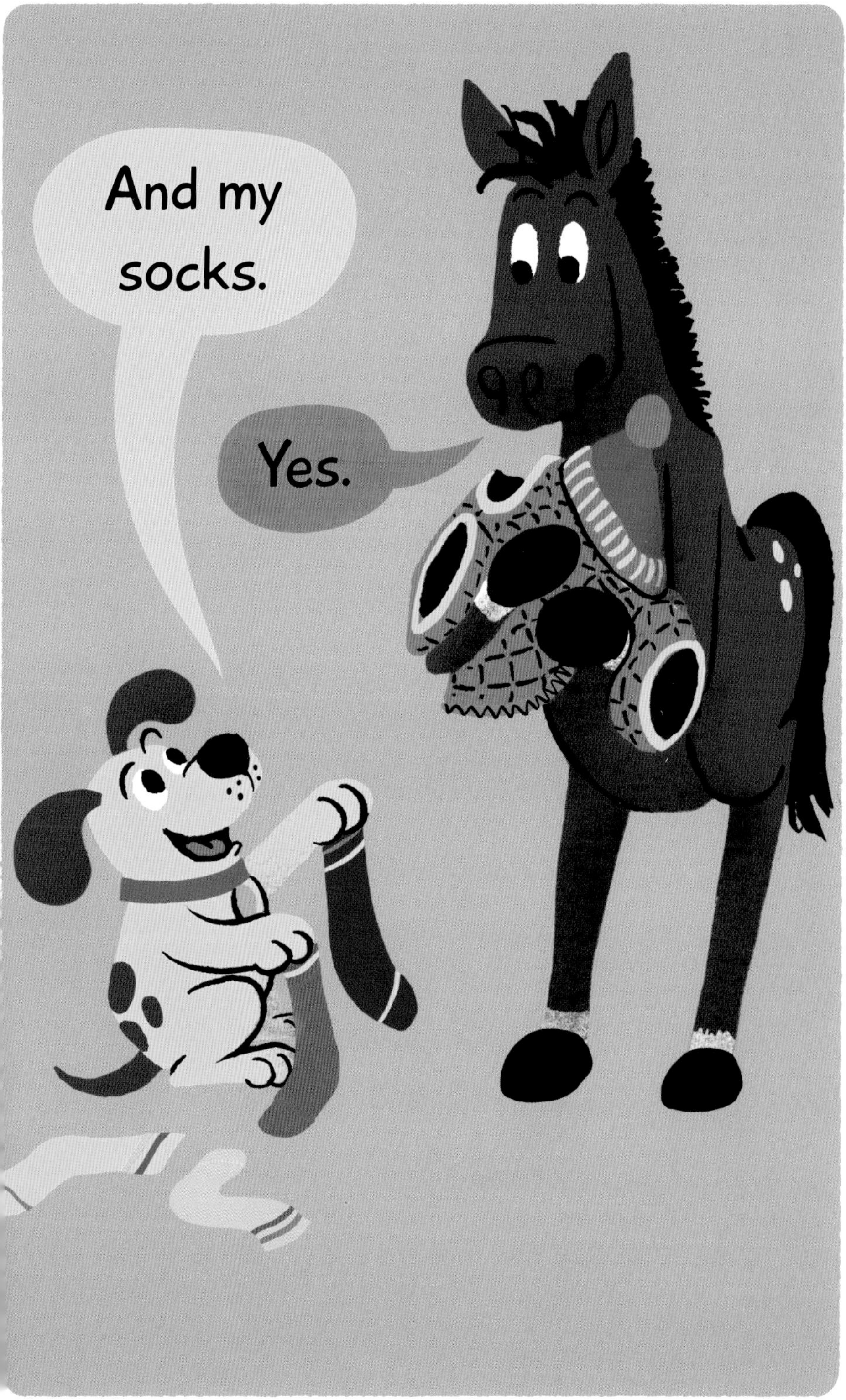
And my socks.
Yes.

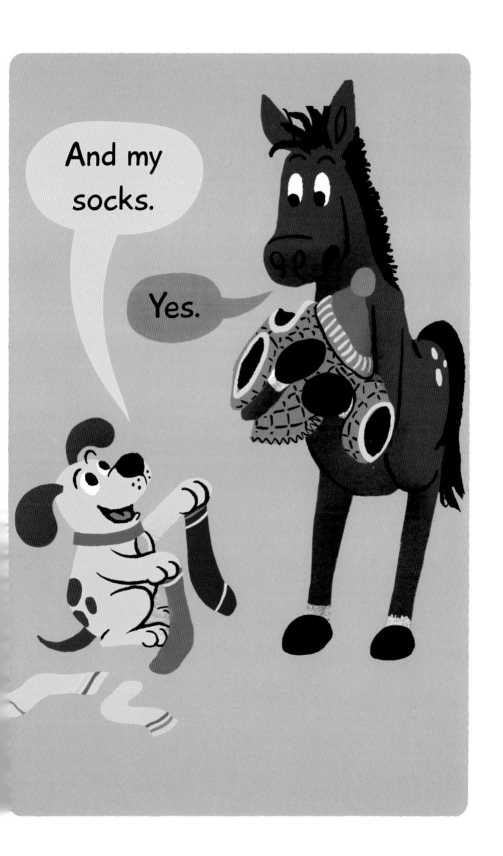

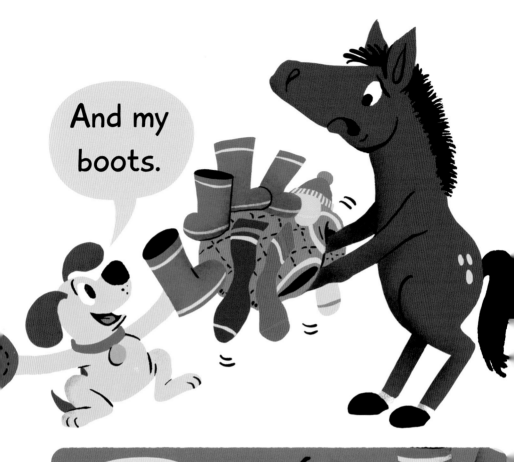

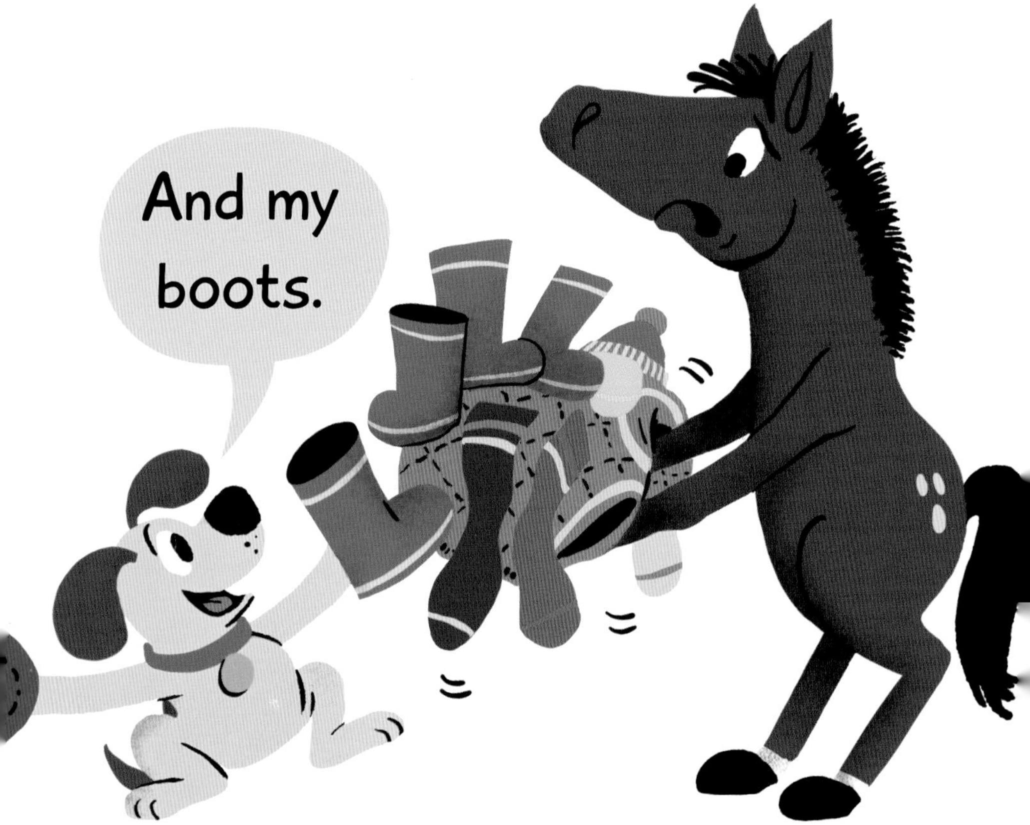
And my boots.

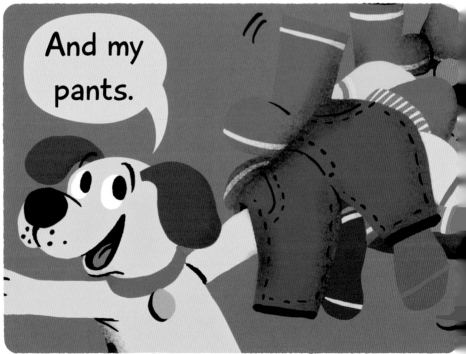

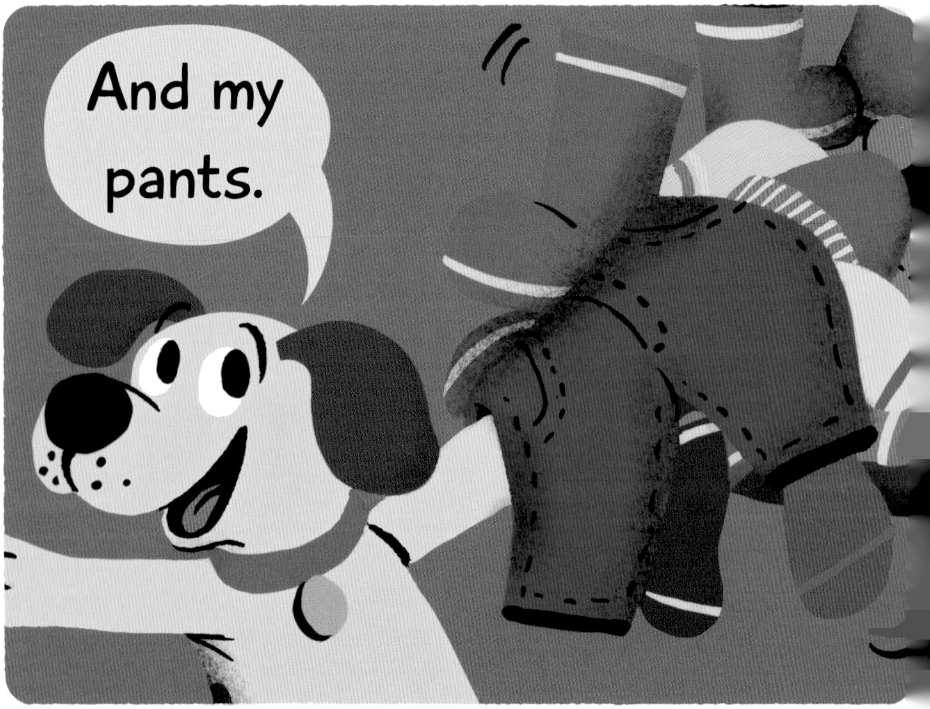
And my pants.

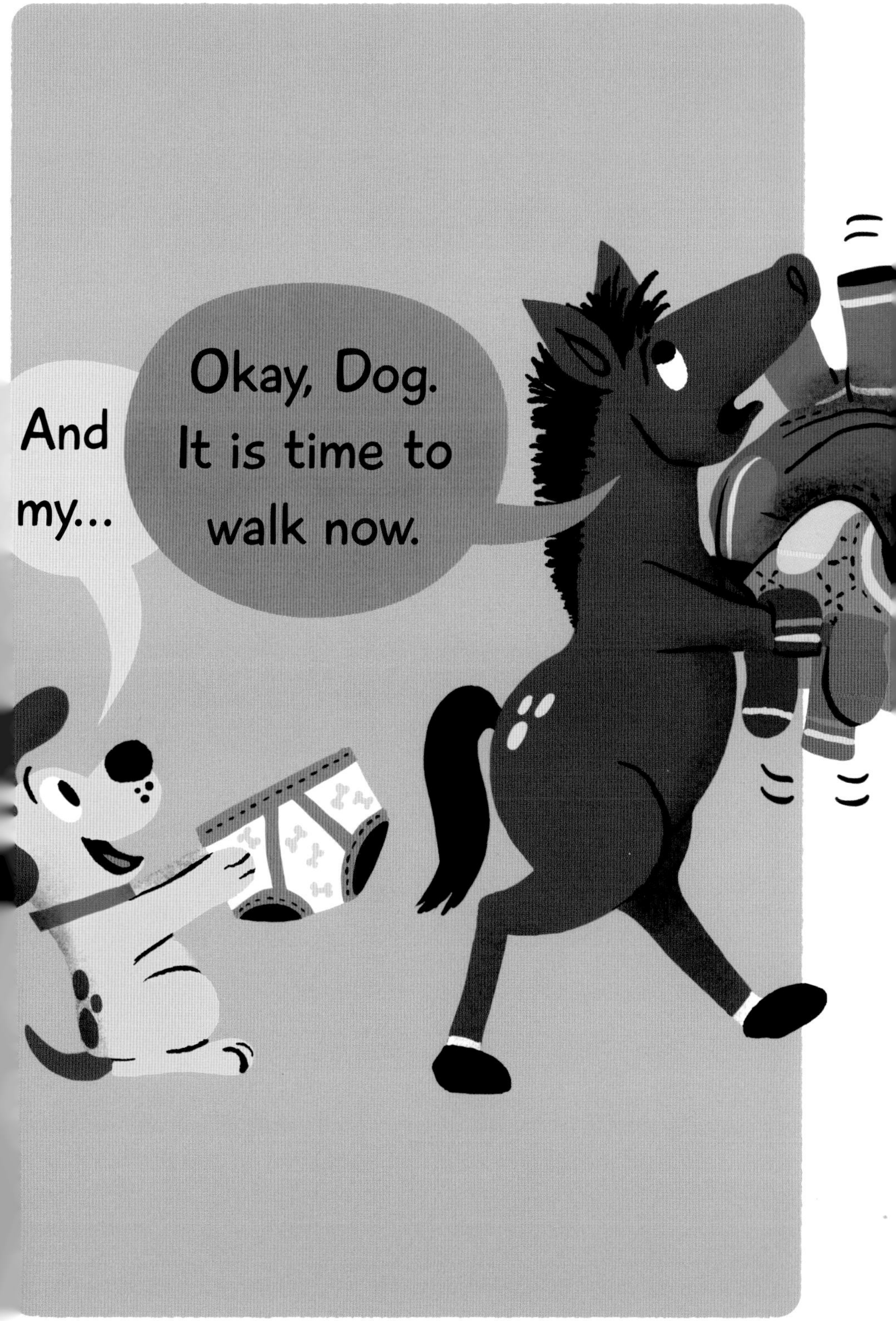
And my...
Okay, Dog. It is time to walk now.

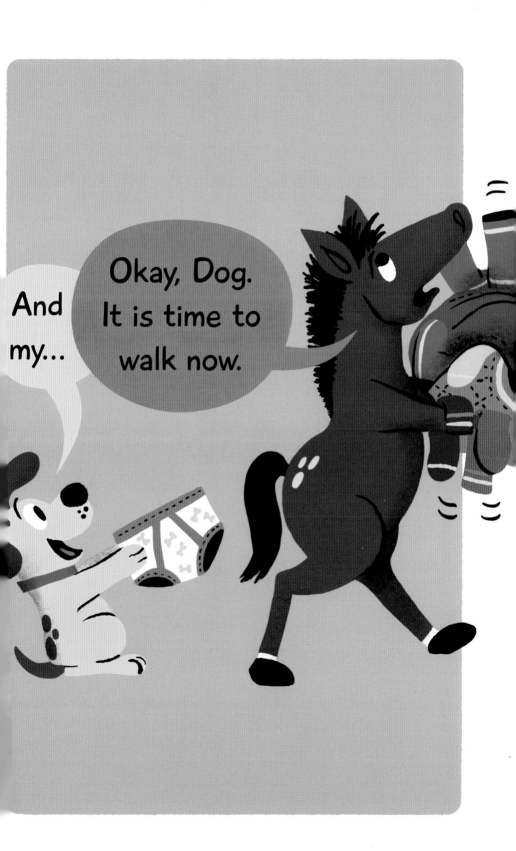

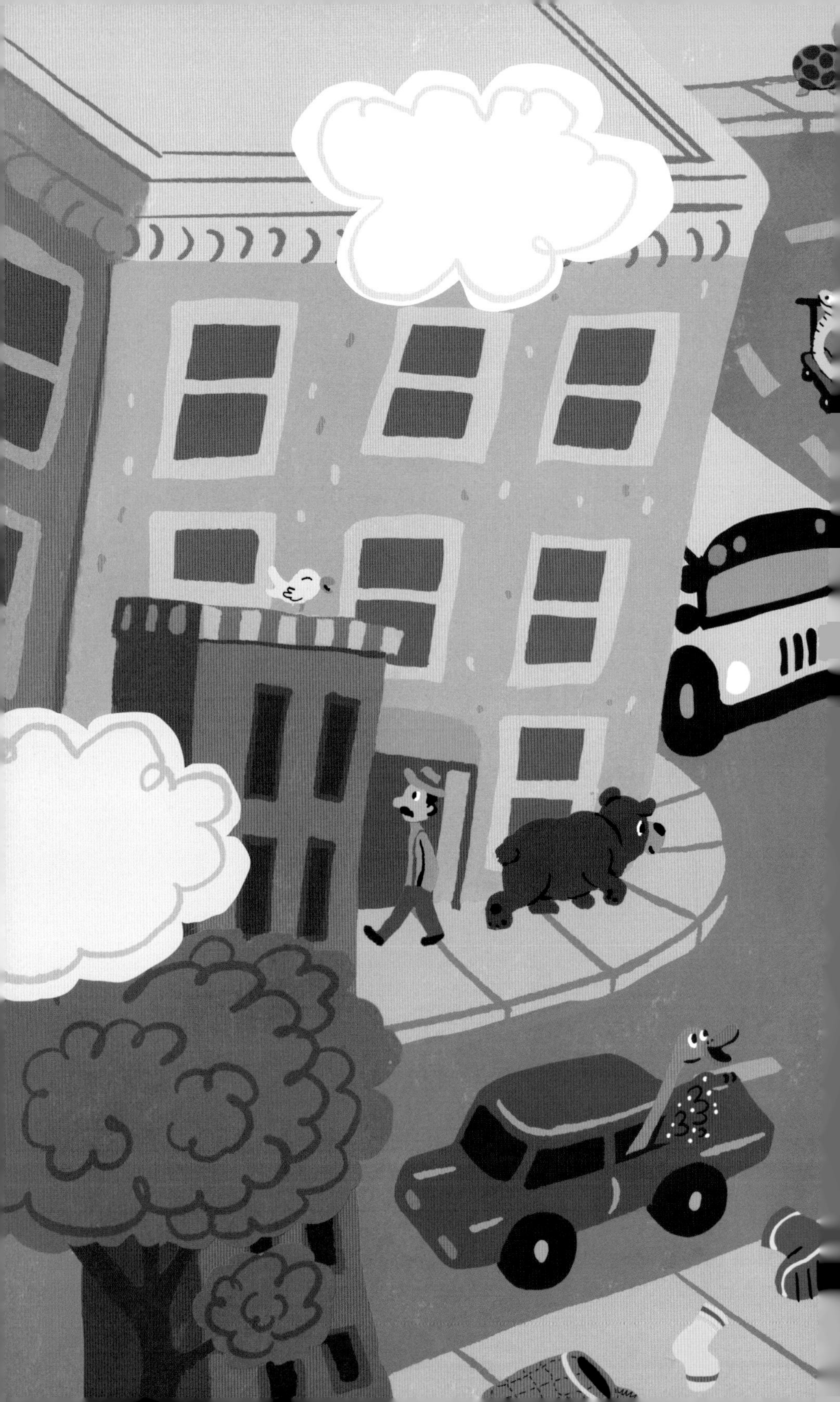

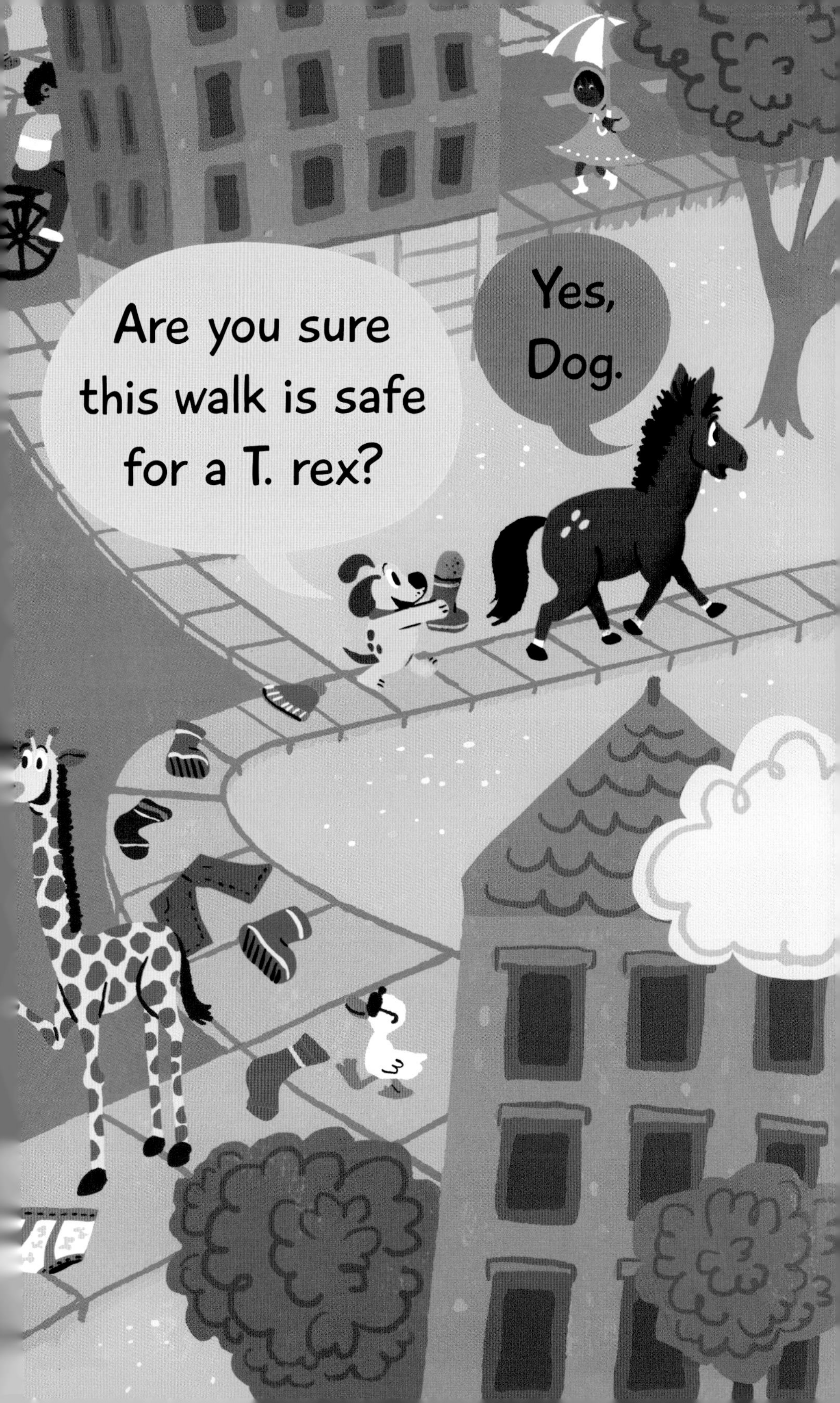
Are you sure this walk is safe for a T. rex?
Yes, Dog.

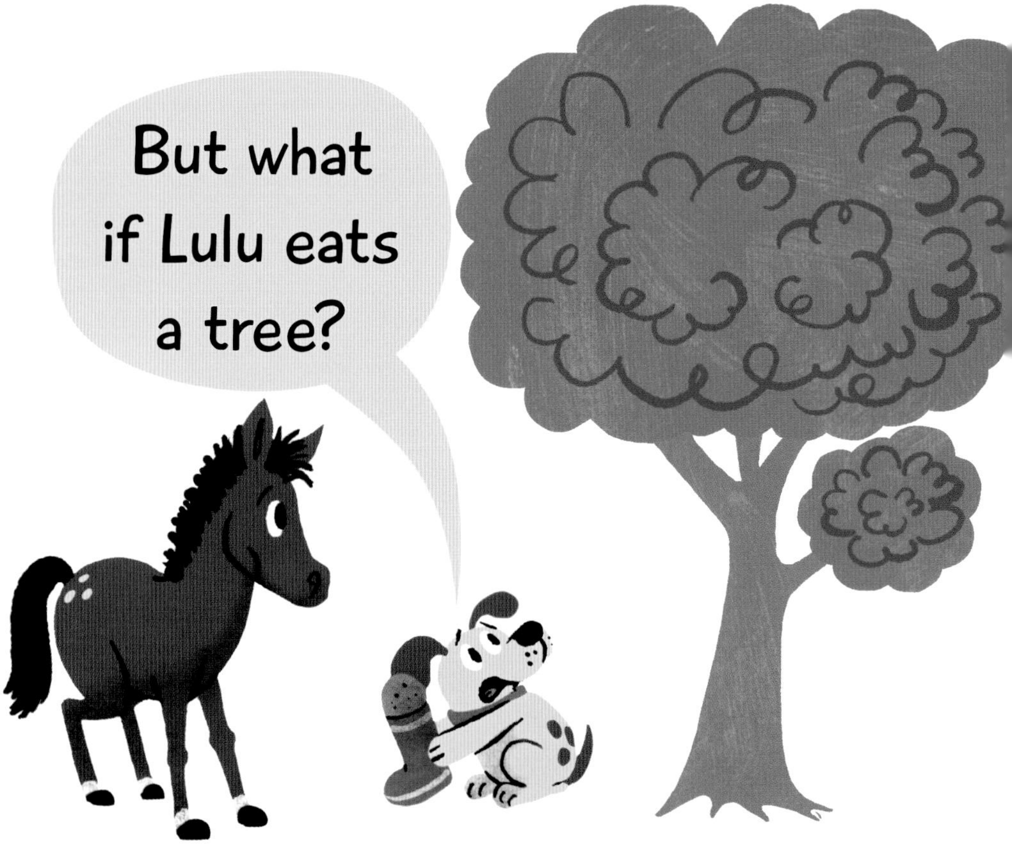
But what if Lulu eats a tree?

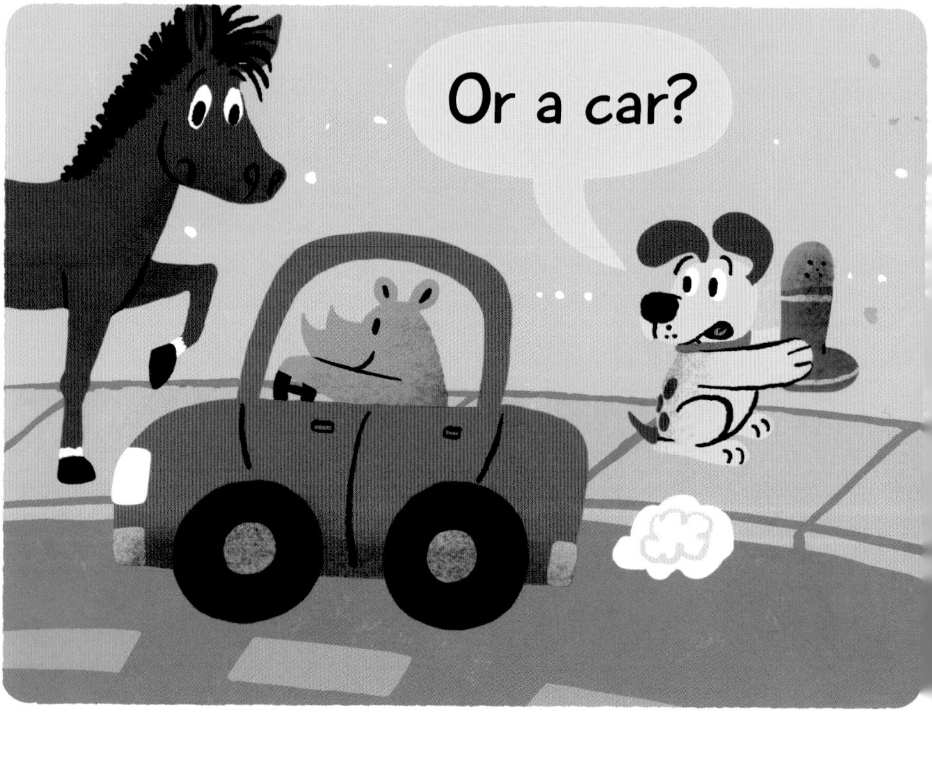
Or a car?

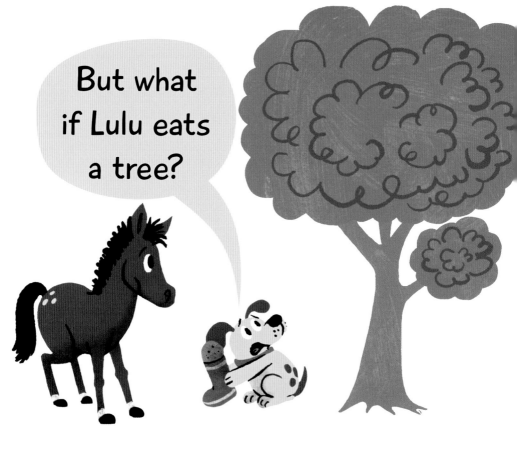

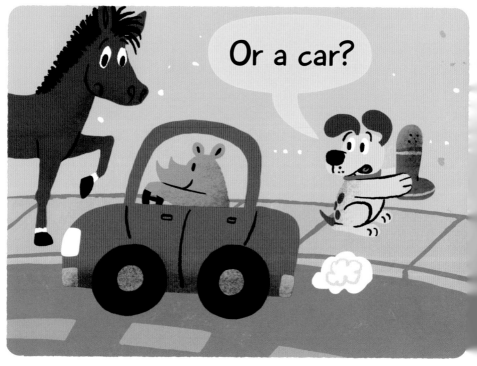

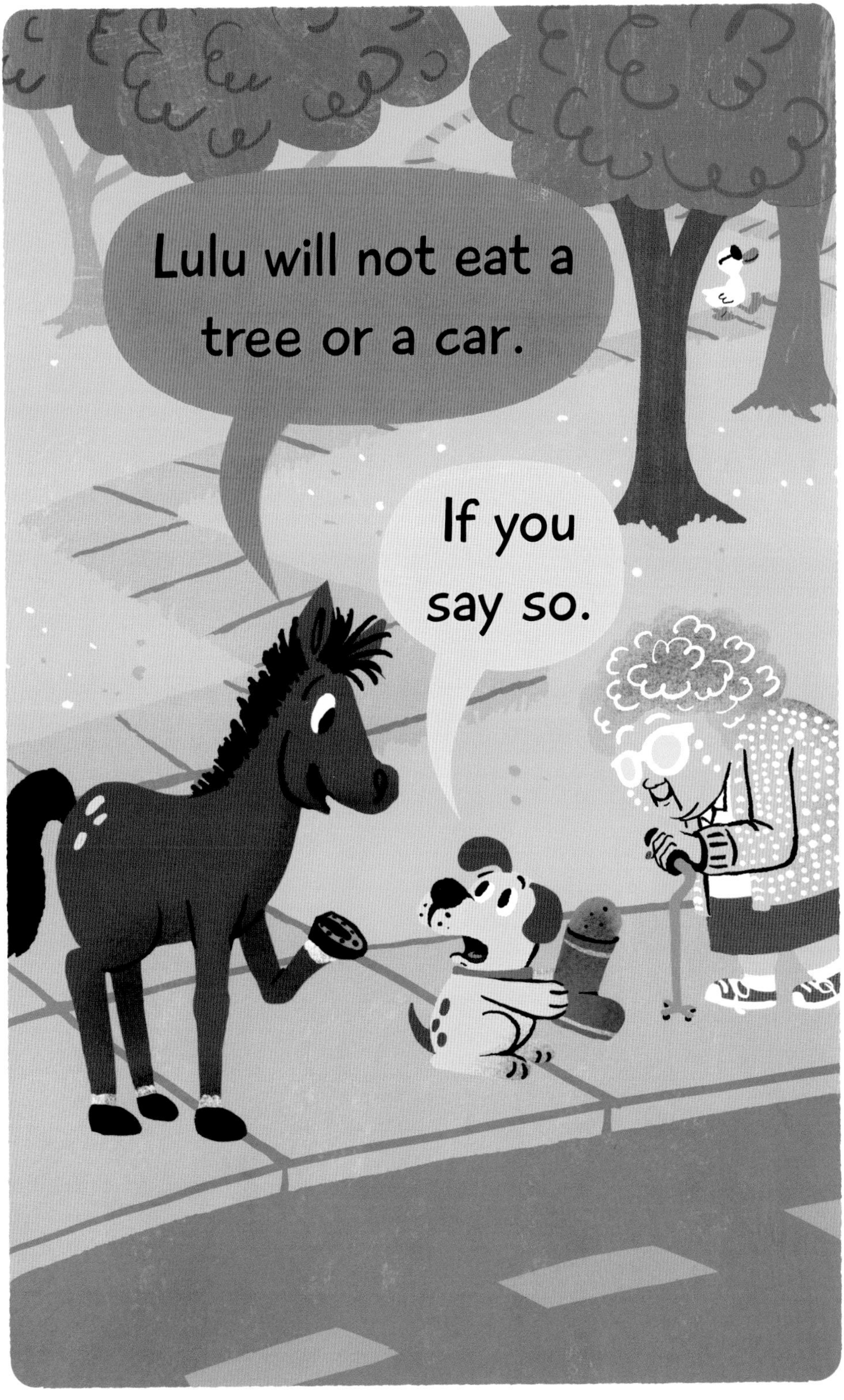
Lulu will not eat a tree or a car.
If you say so.

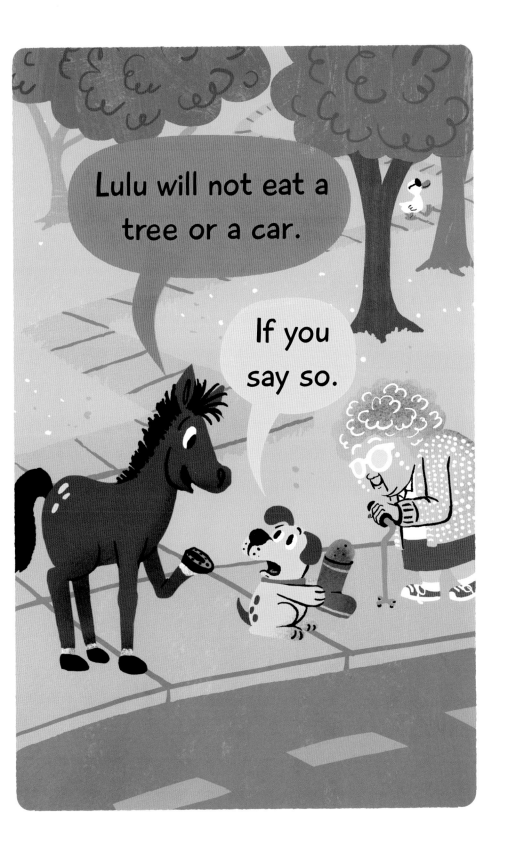

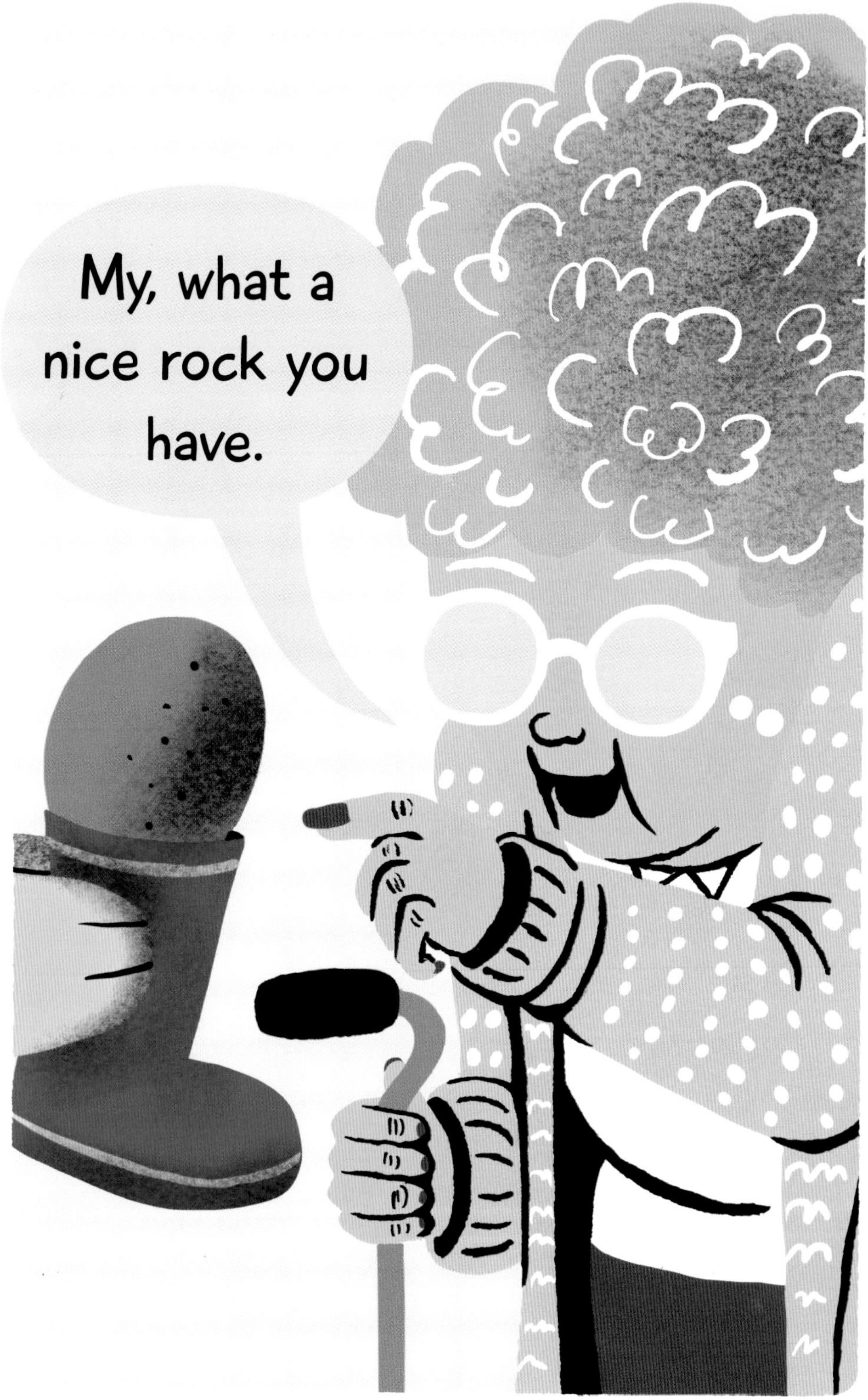
My, what a nice rock you have.

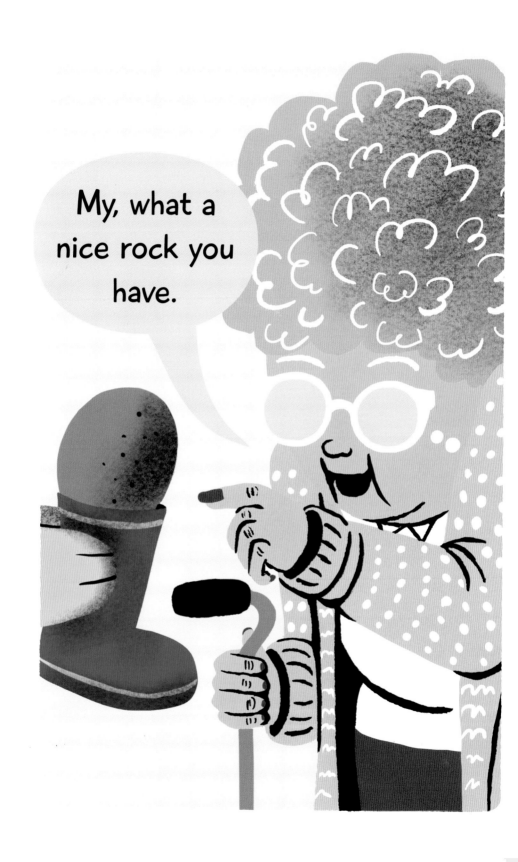

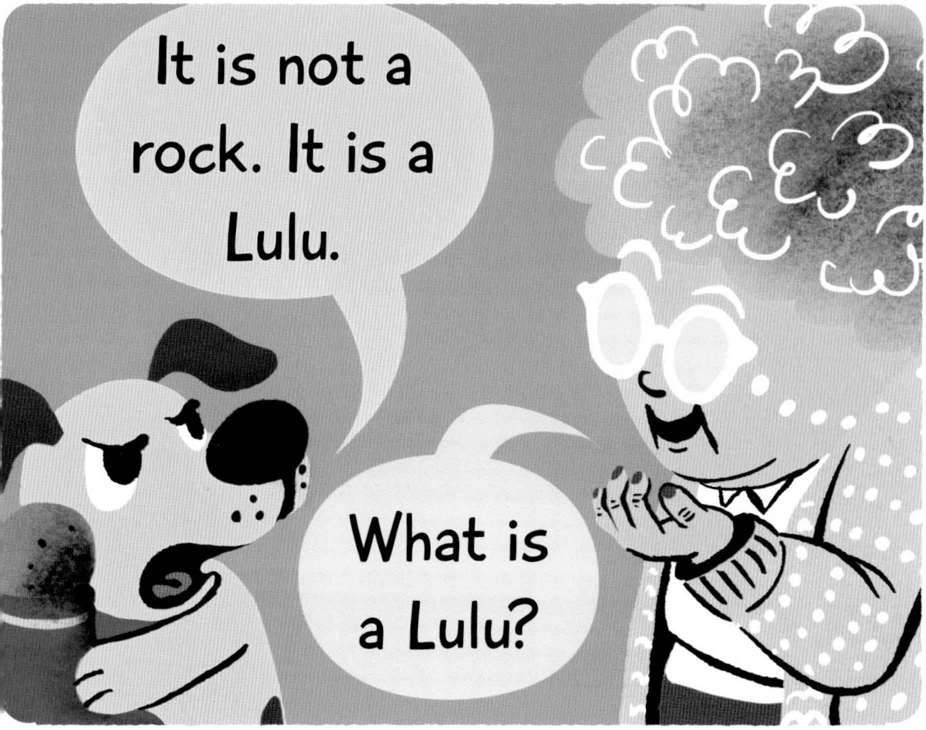
It is not a rock. It is a Lulu.
What is a Lulu?

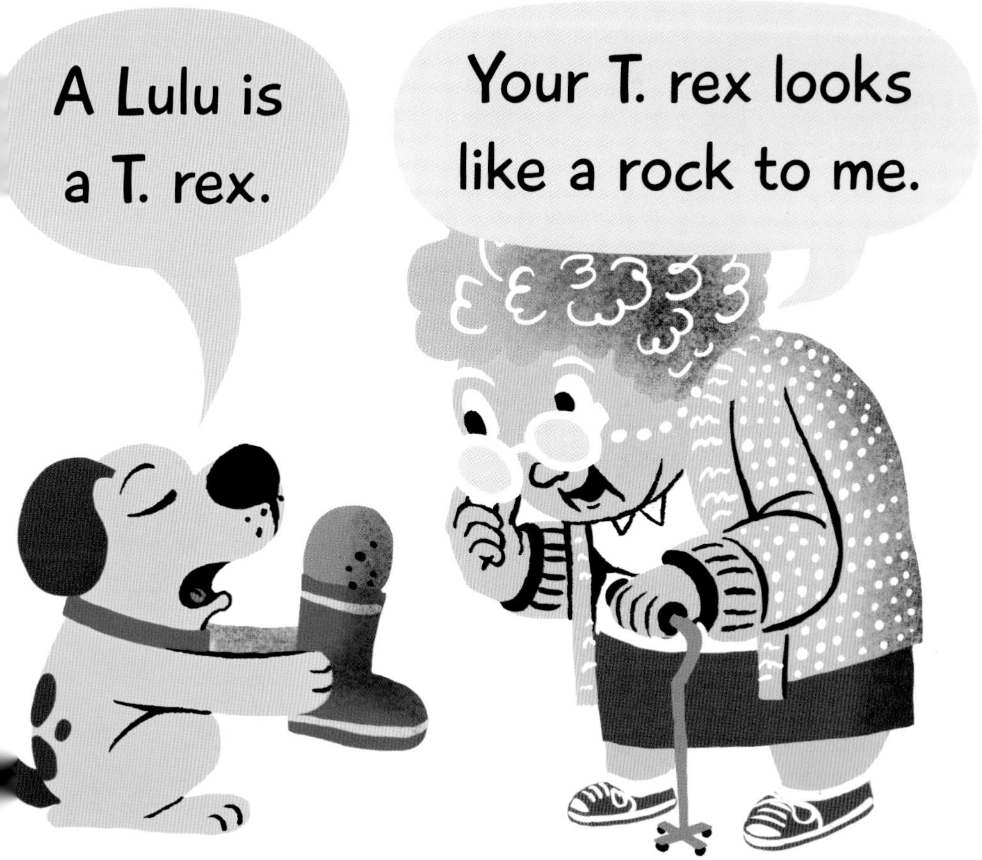
A Lulu is a T. rex.
Your T. rex looks like a rock to me.

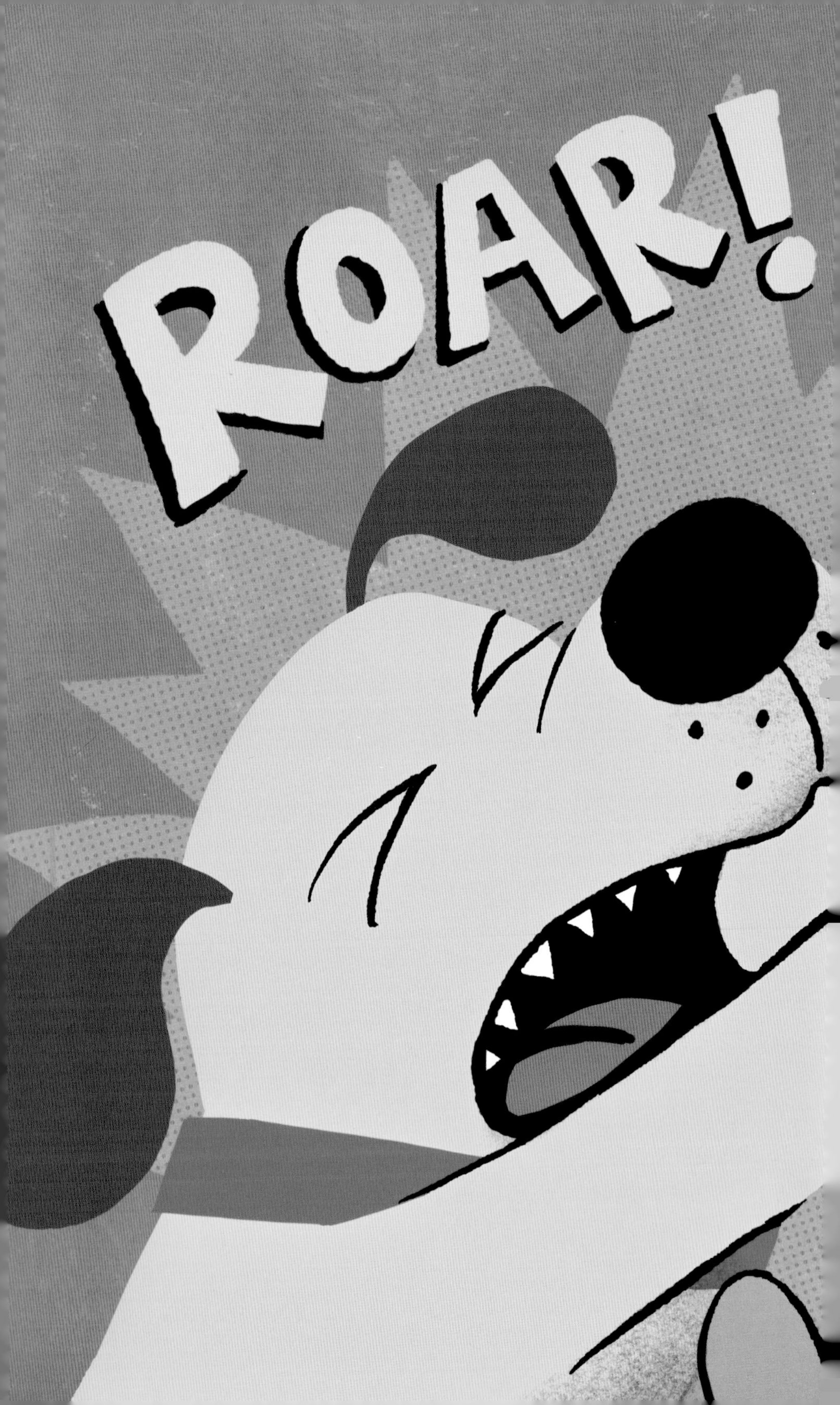
ROAR!

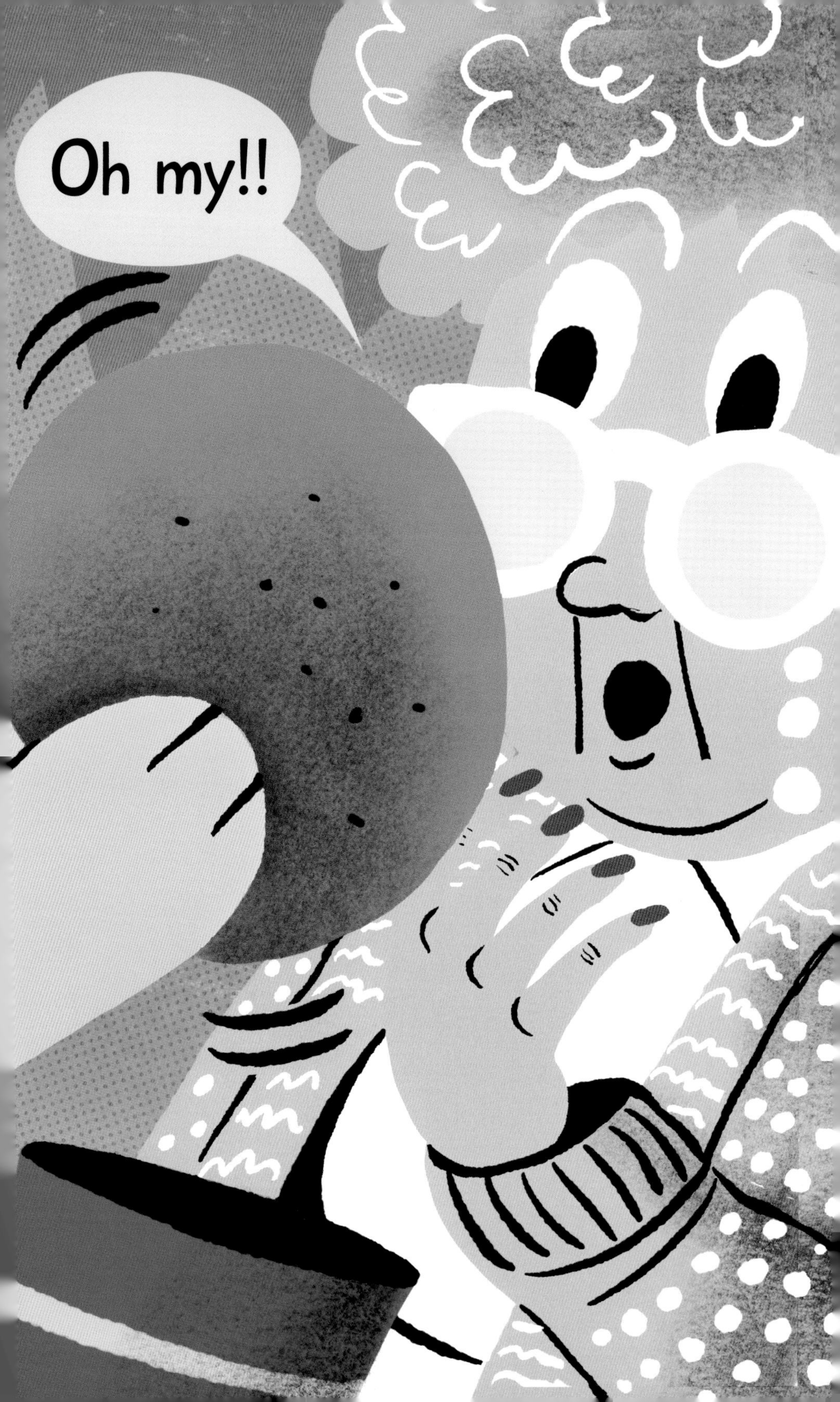
Oh my!!

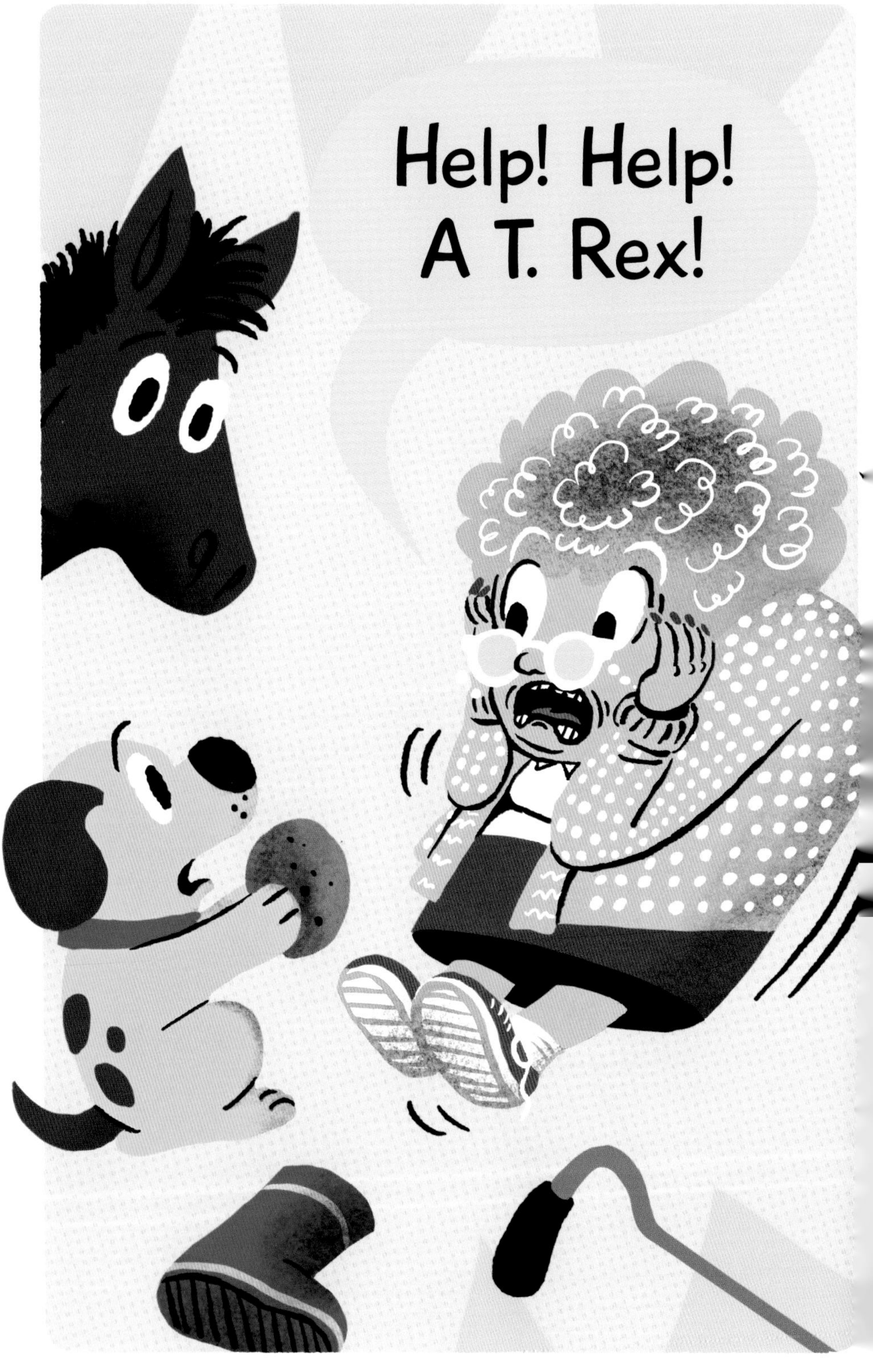
Help! Help! A T. Rex!

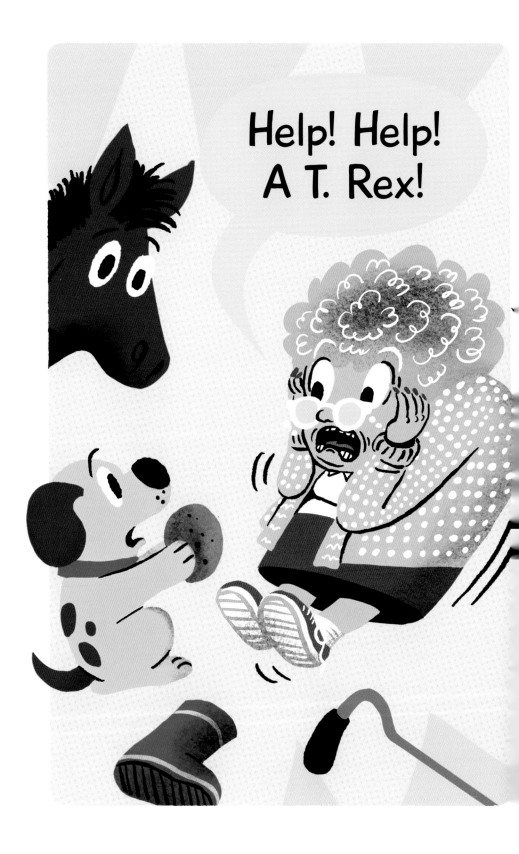

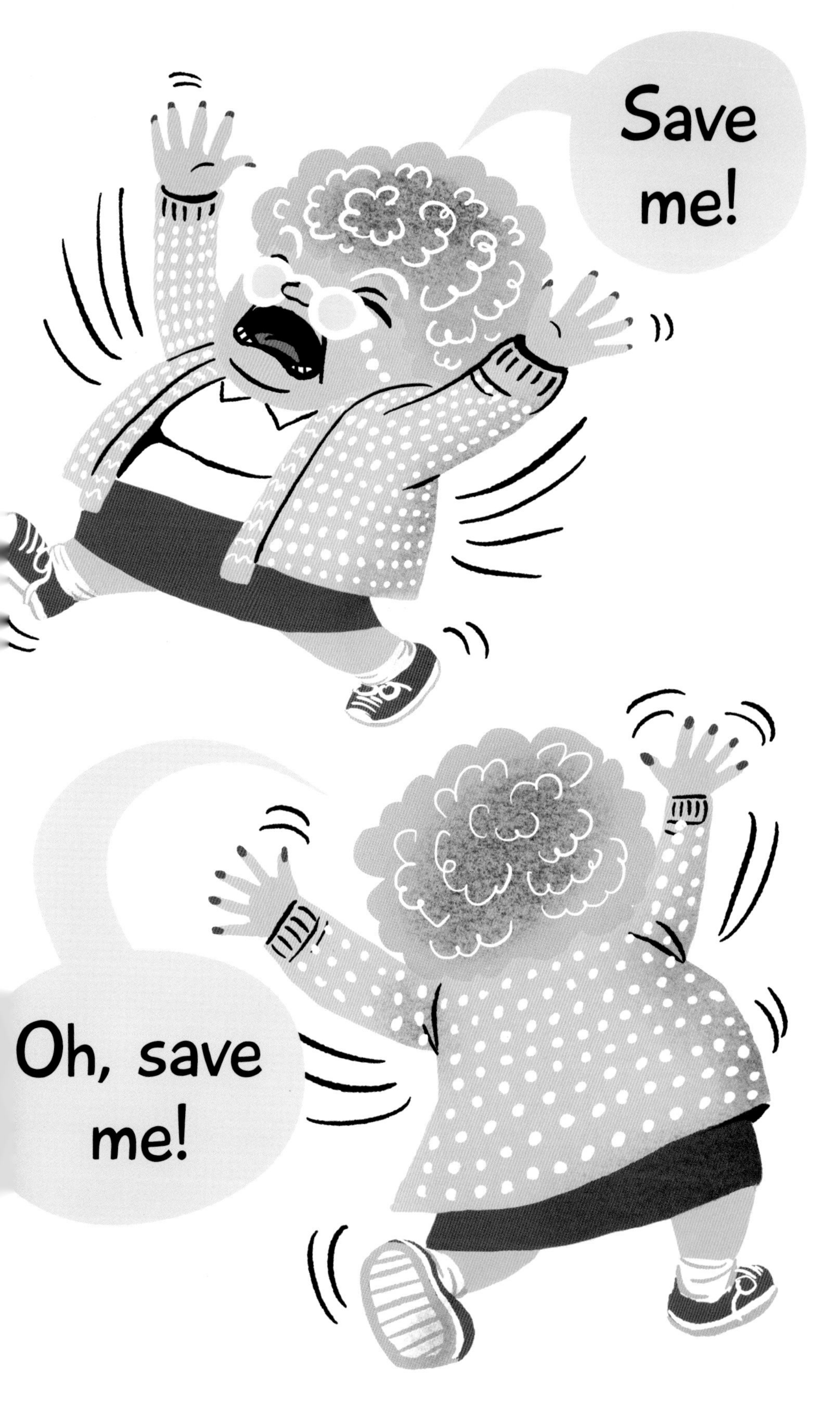
Save me!
Oh, save me!

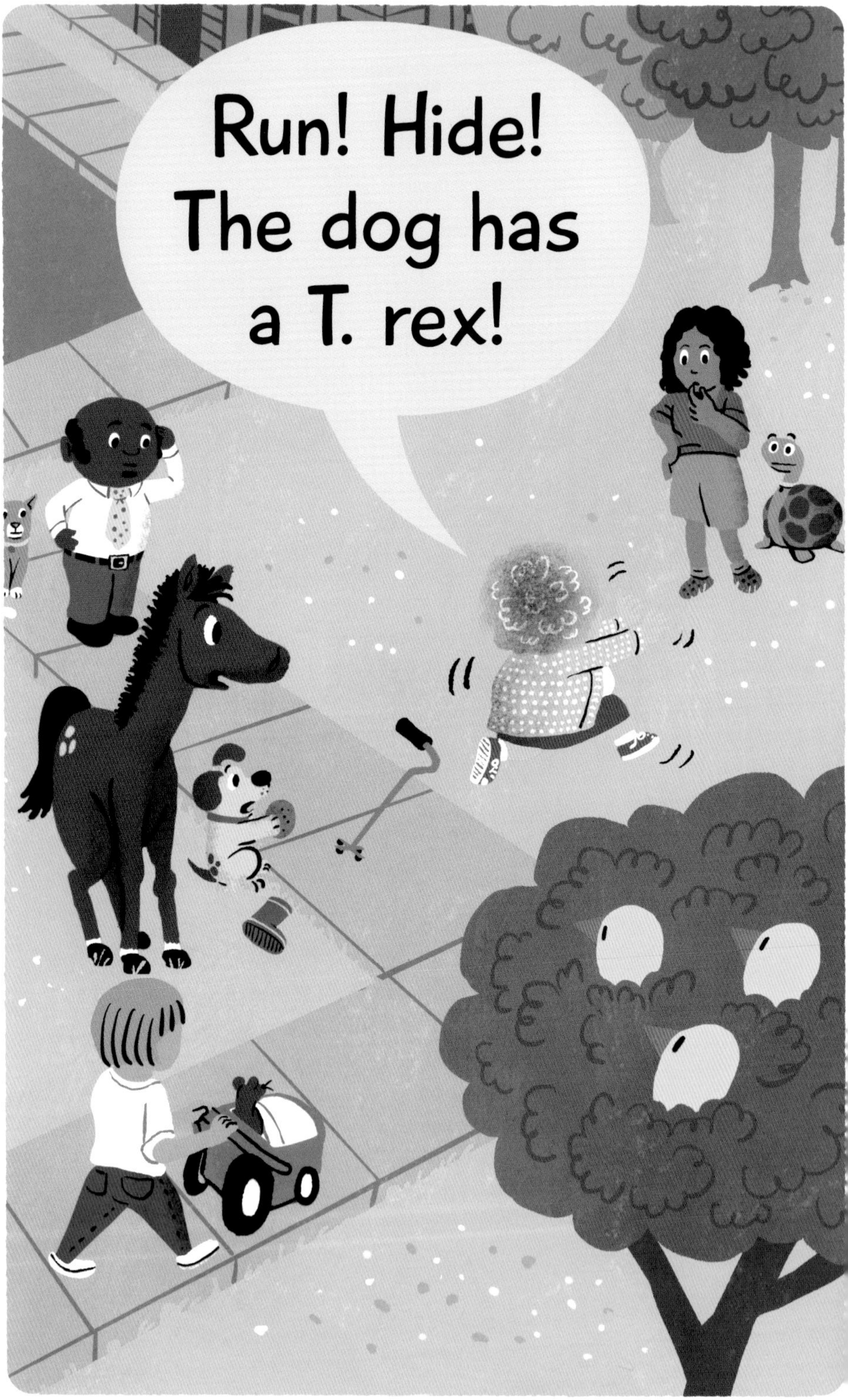
Run! Hide! The dog has a T. rex!

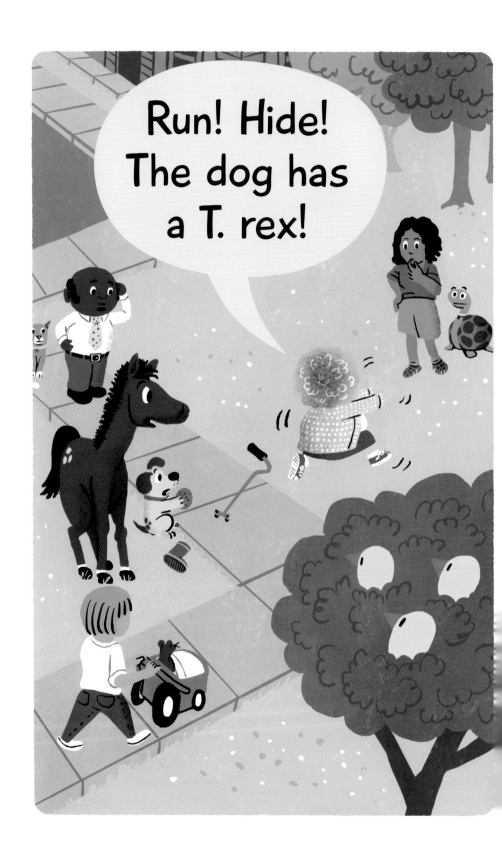

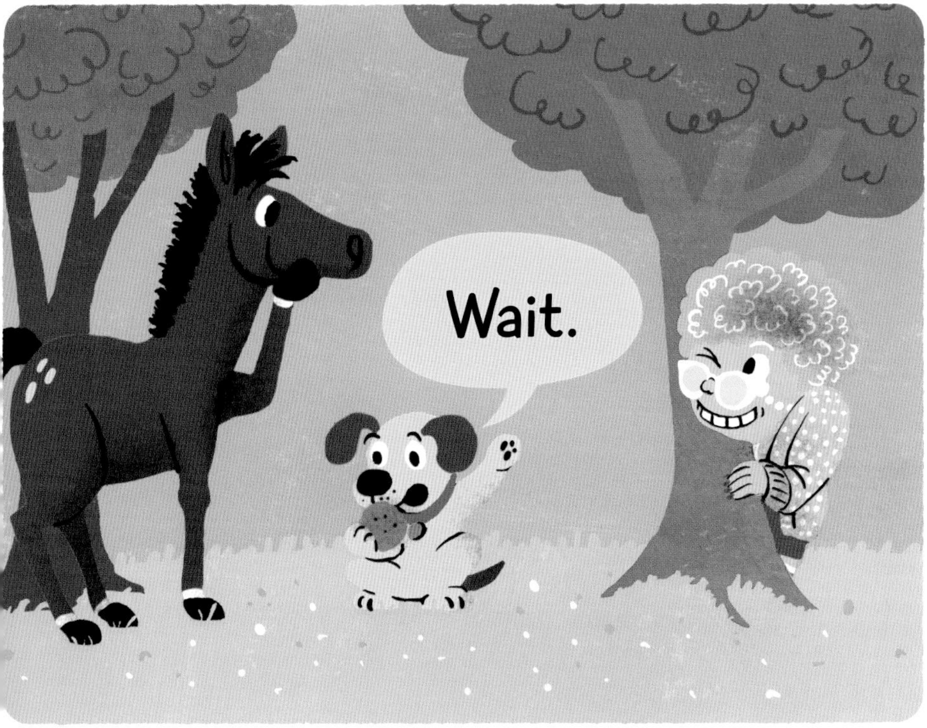
Wait.

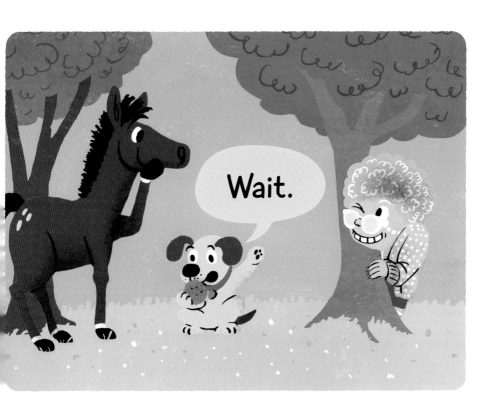

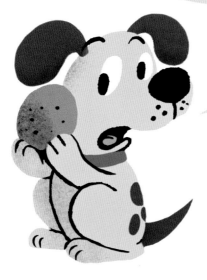

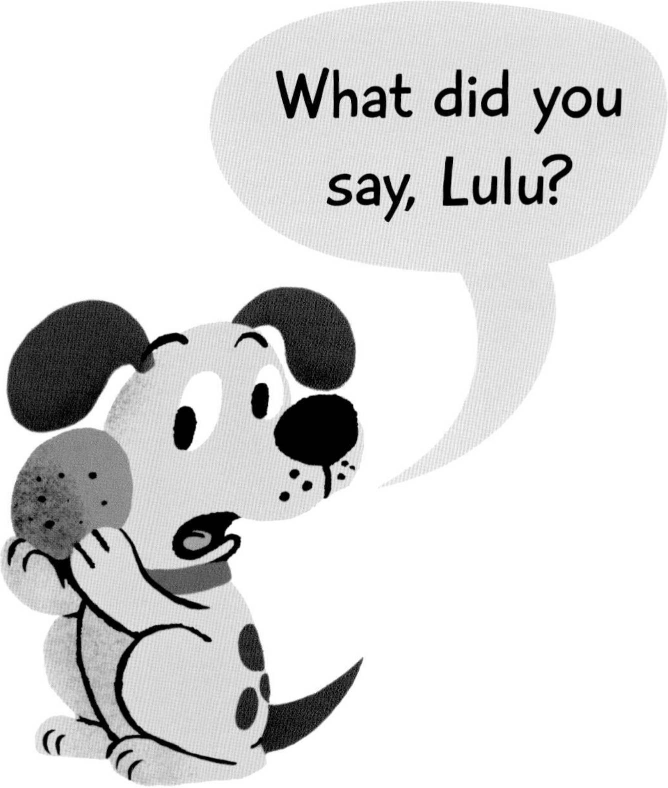
What did you say, Lulu?

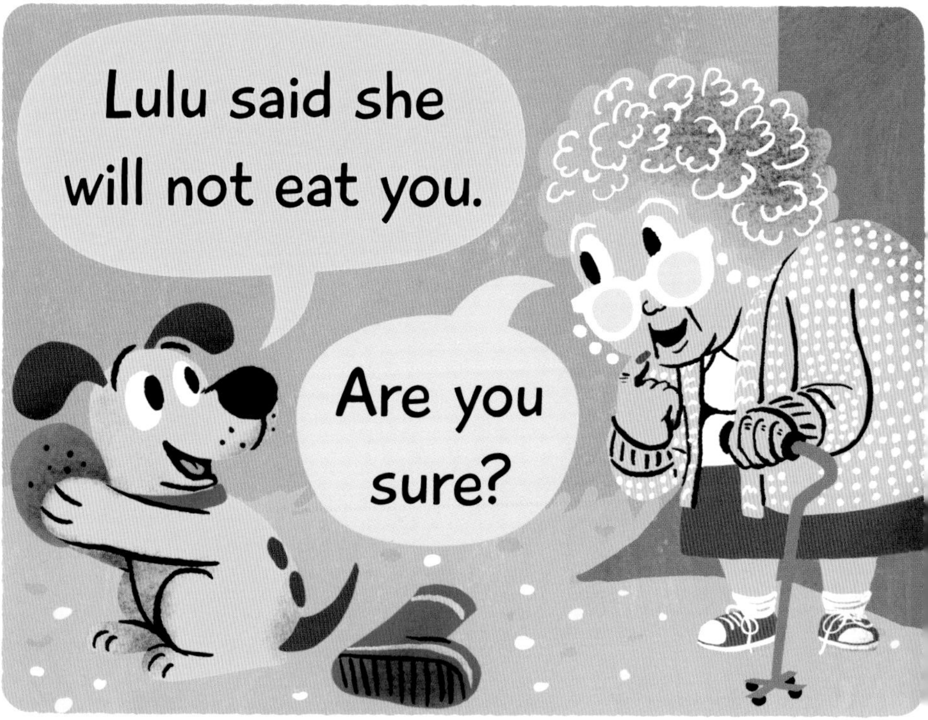
Lulu said she will not eat you.
Are you sure?

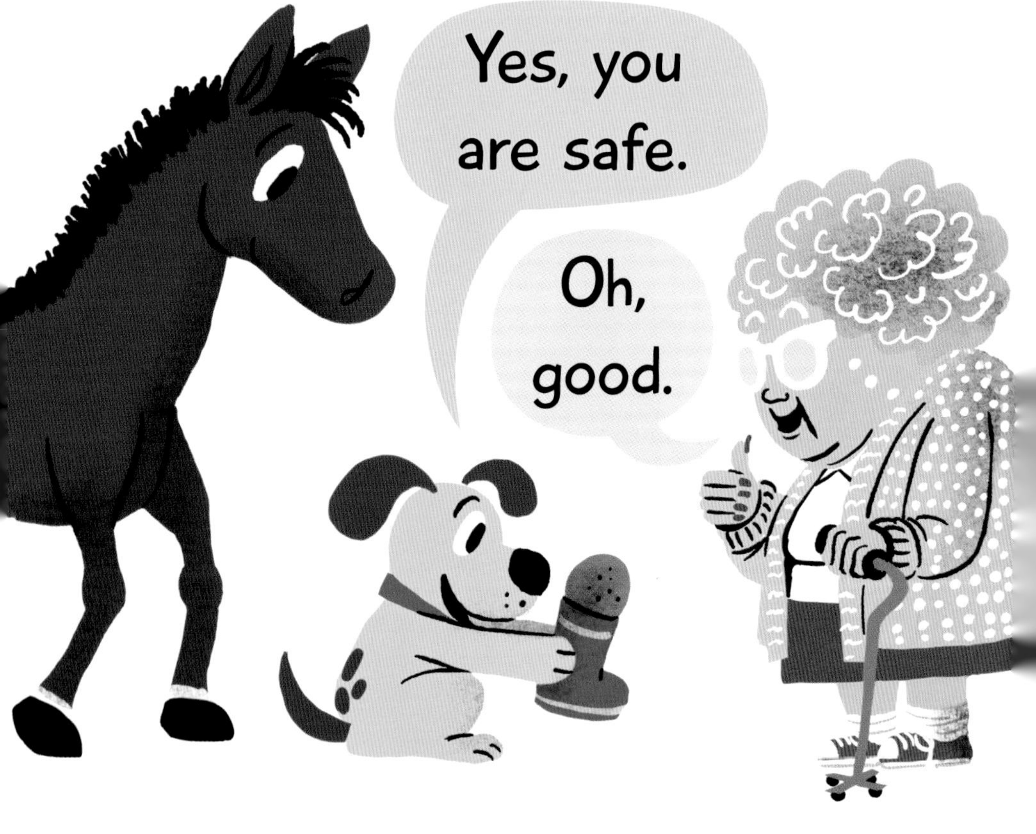
Yes, you are safe.
Oh, good.

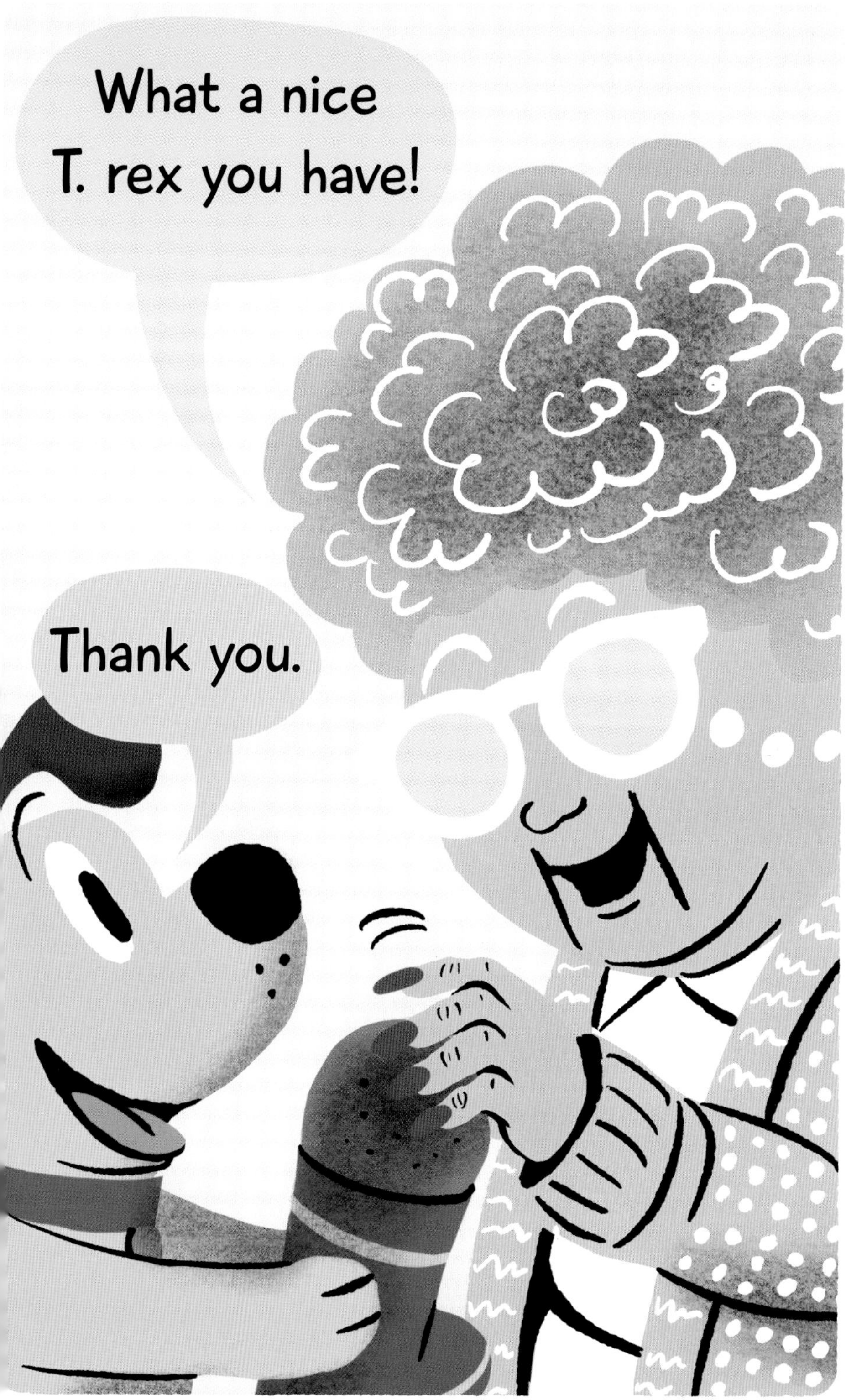
What a nice
T. rex you have!
Thank you.

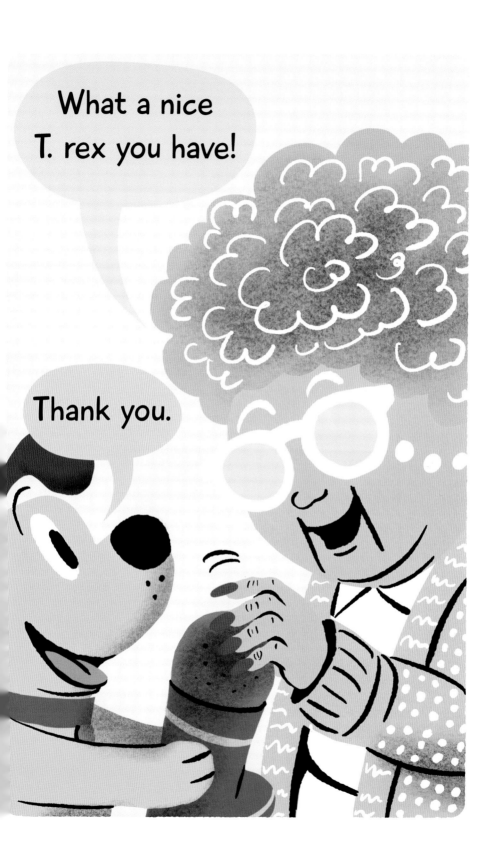

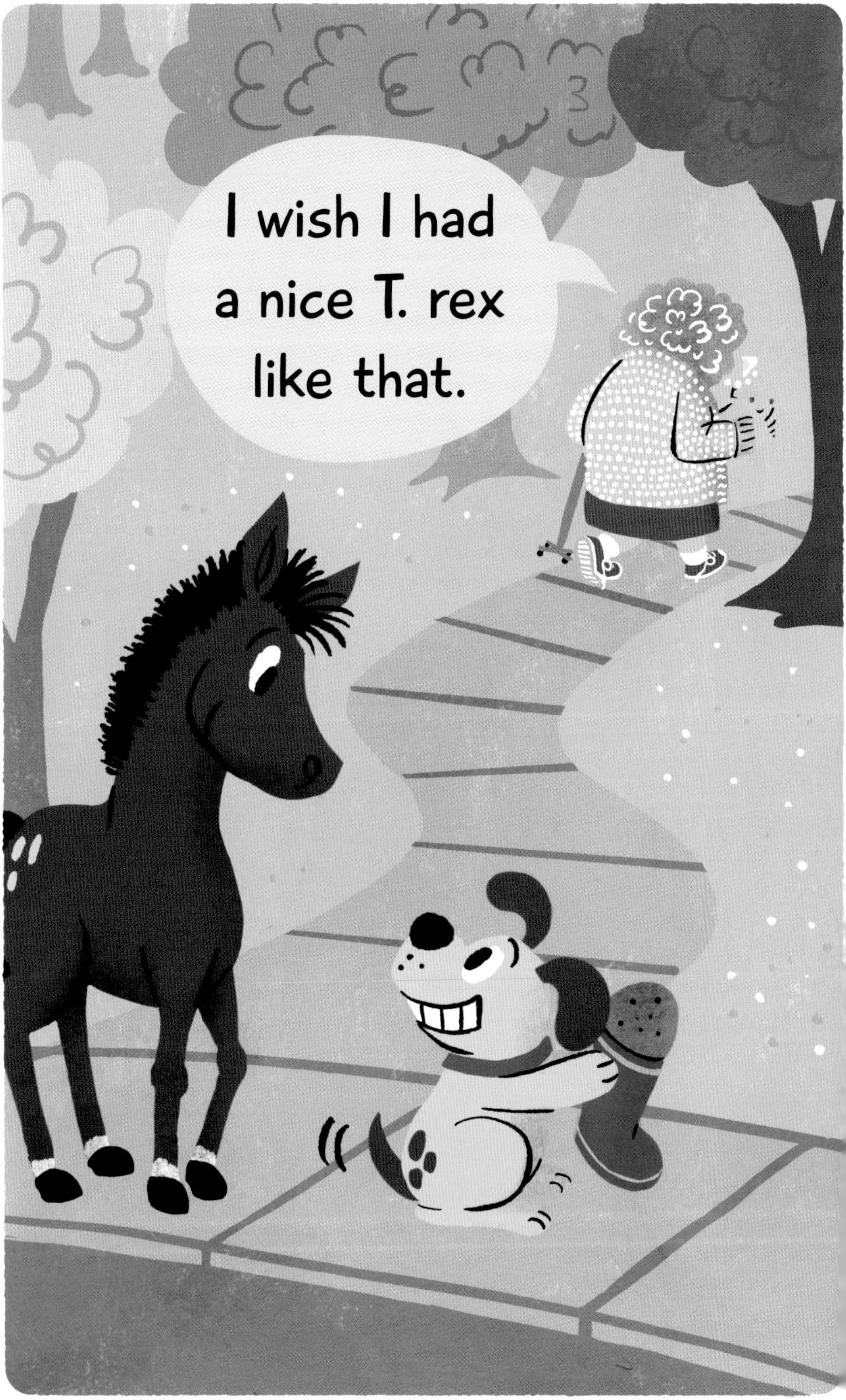
I wish I had
a nice T. rex
like that.

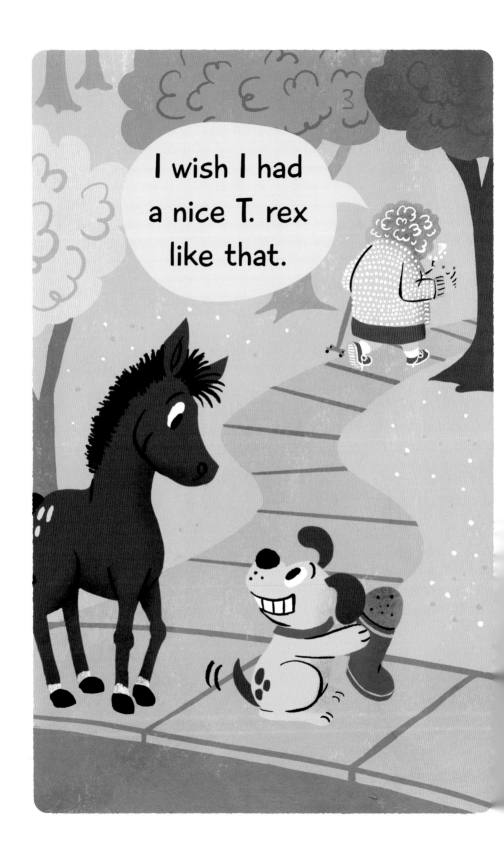

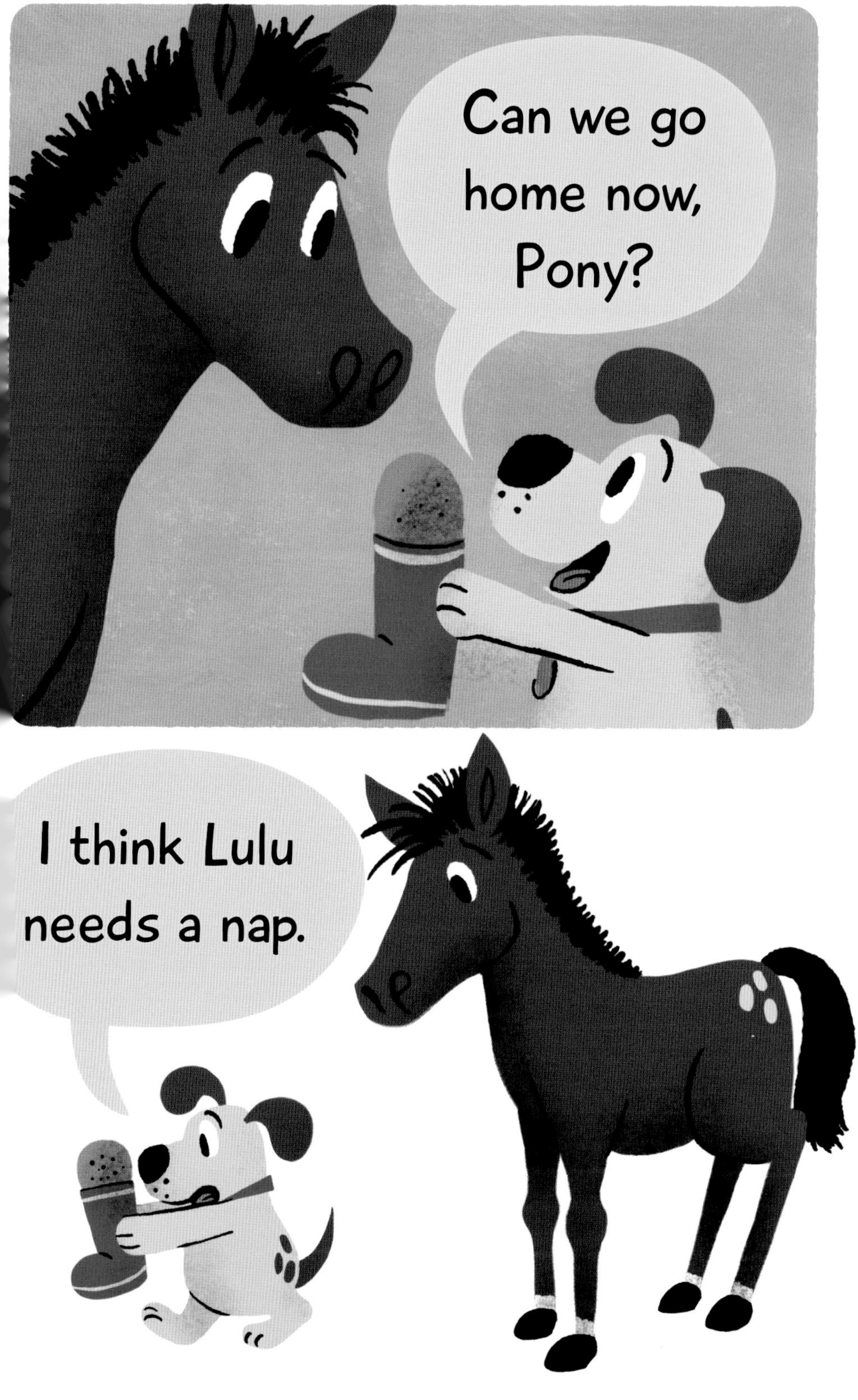
Can we go home now, Pony?
I think Lulu needs a nap.

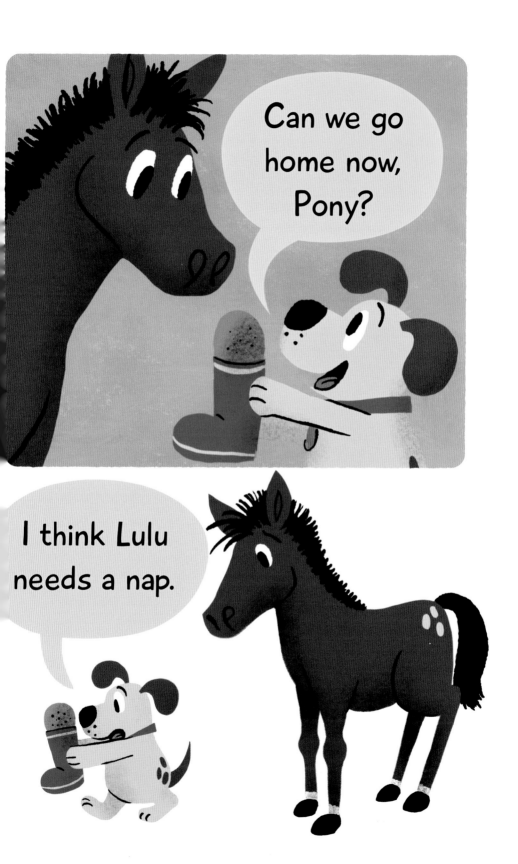

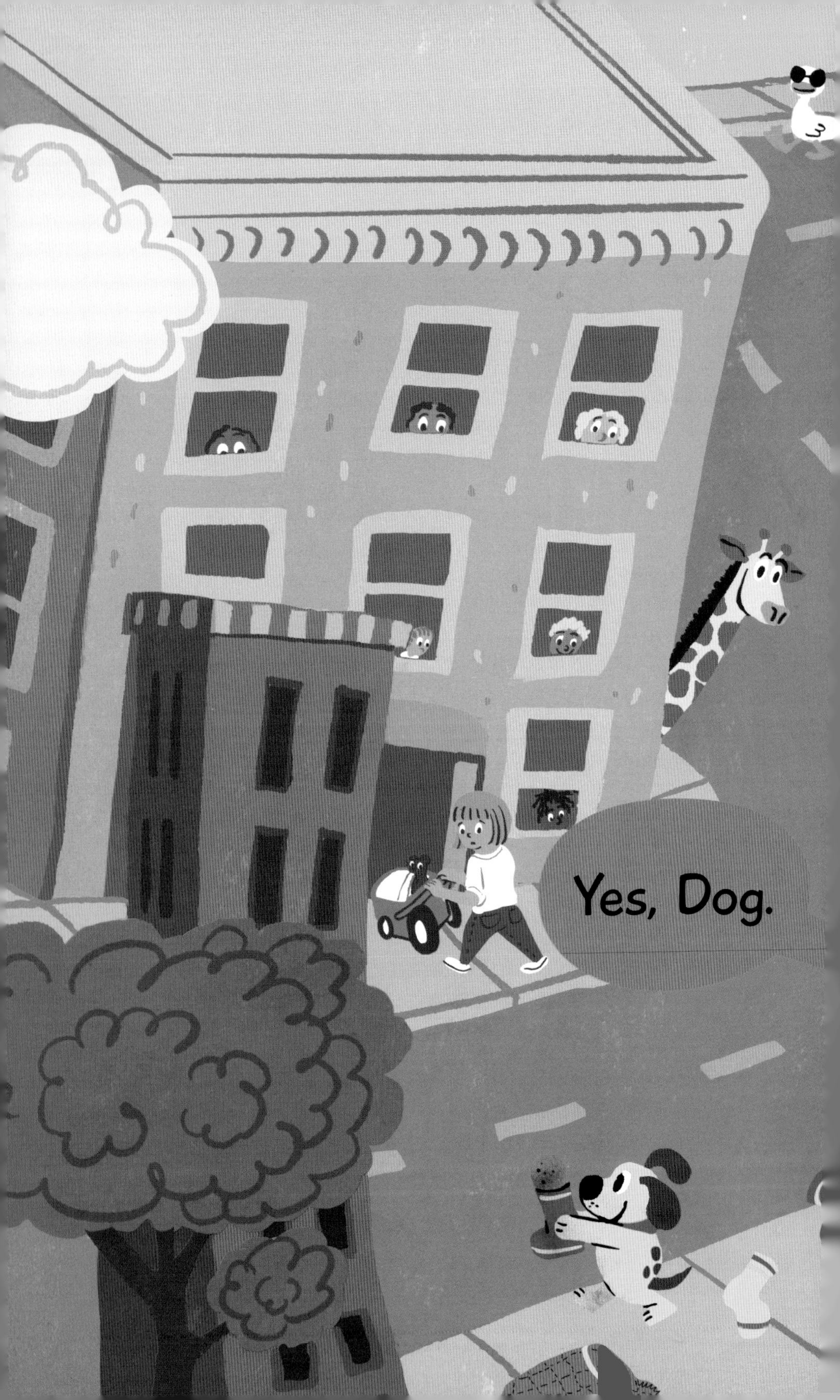
Yes, Dog.

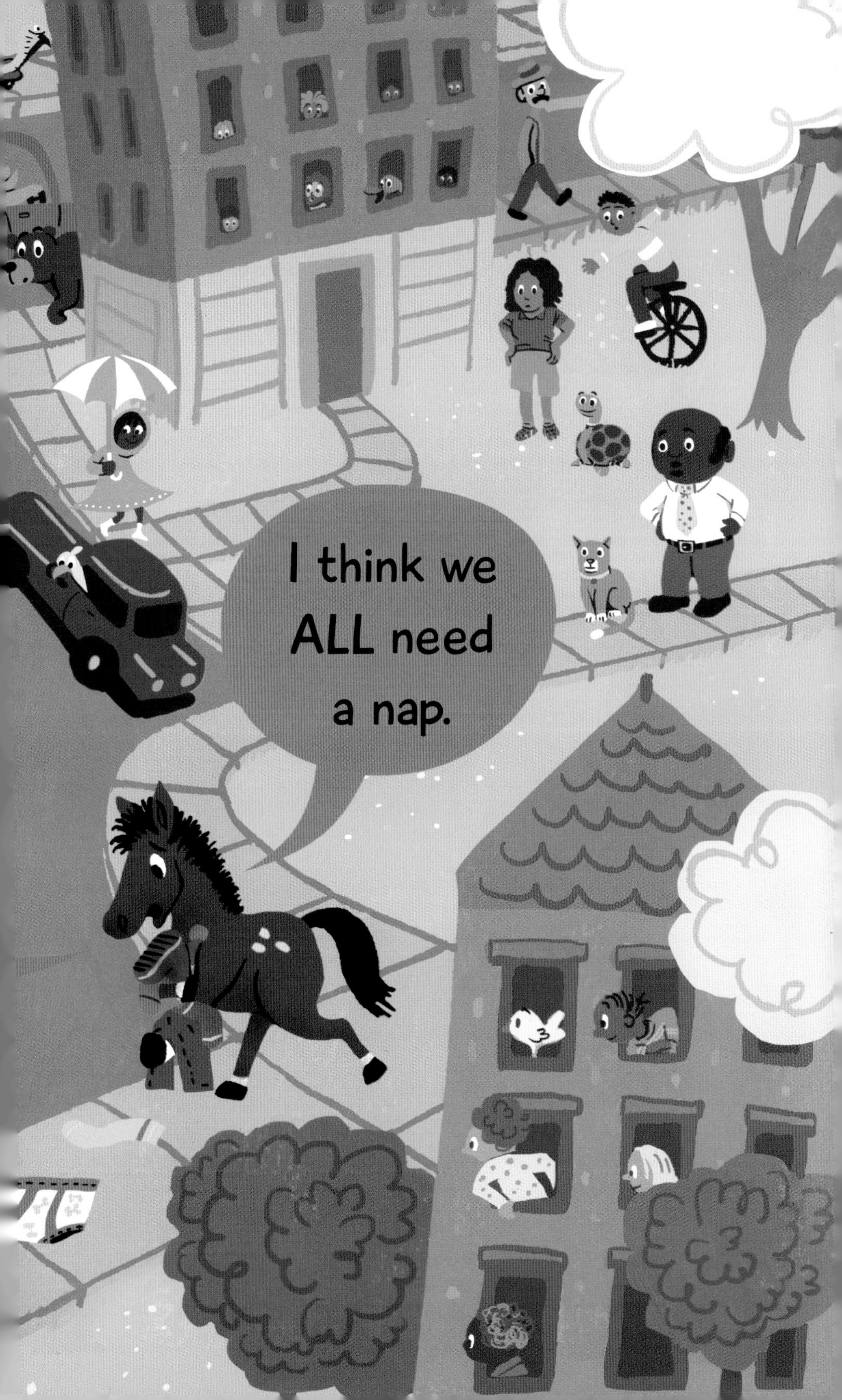
I think we ALL need a nap.

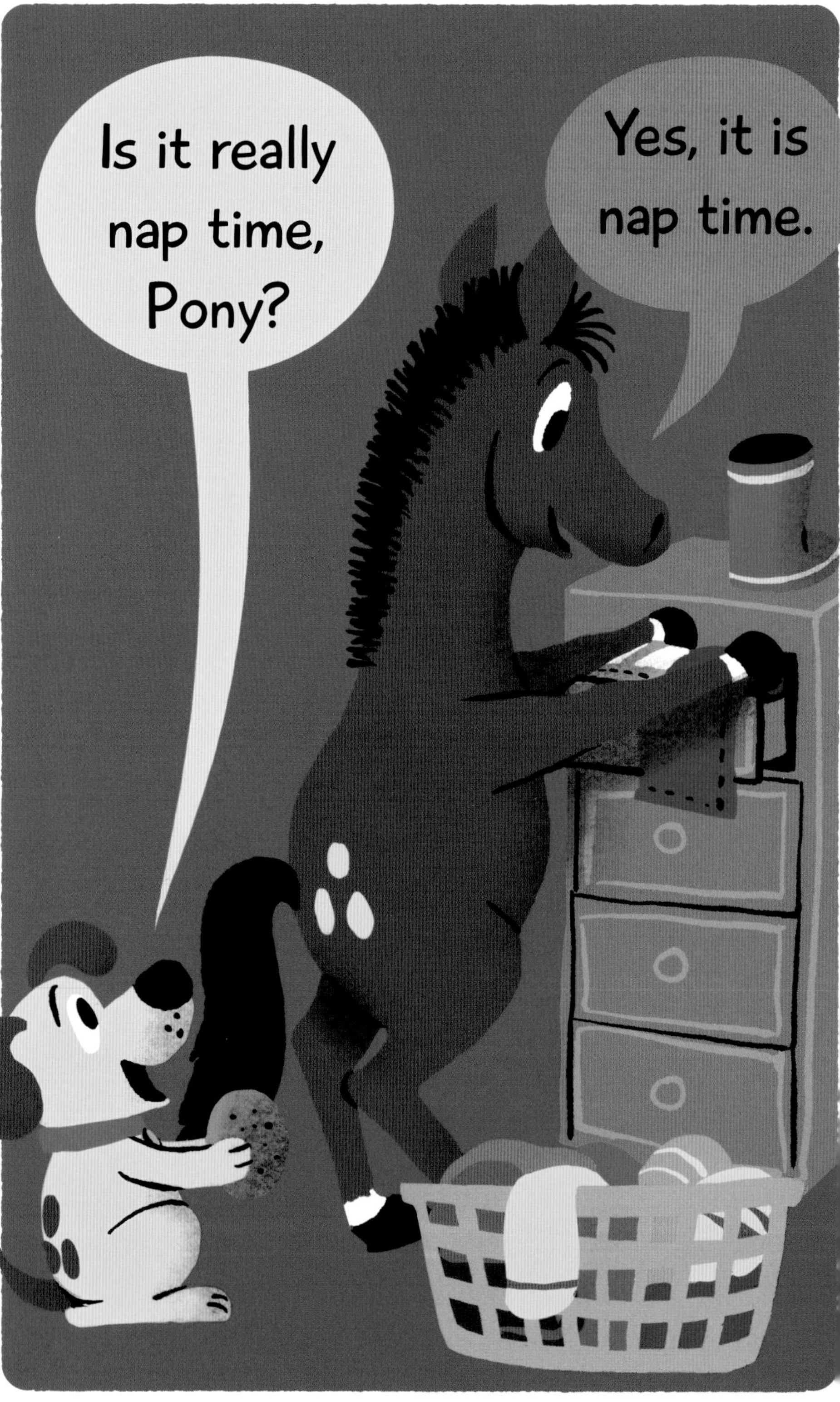
Is it really nap time, Pony?
Yes, it is nap time.

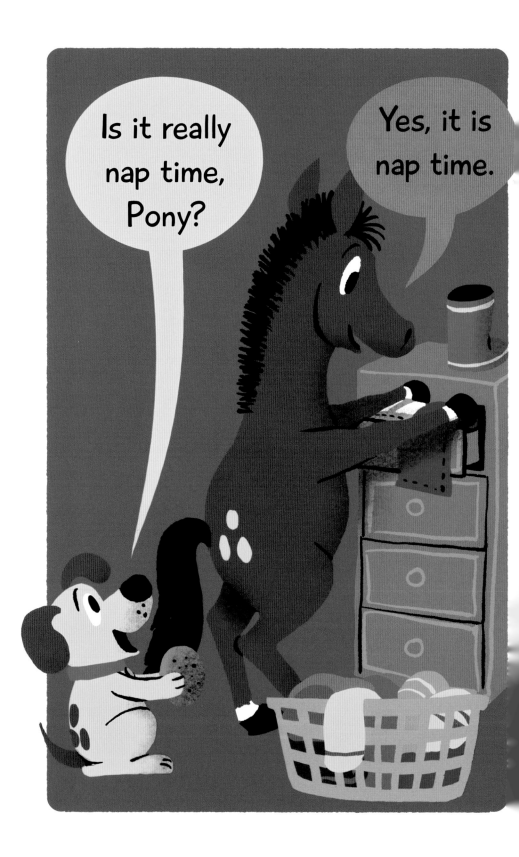

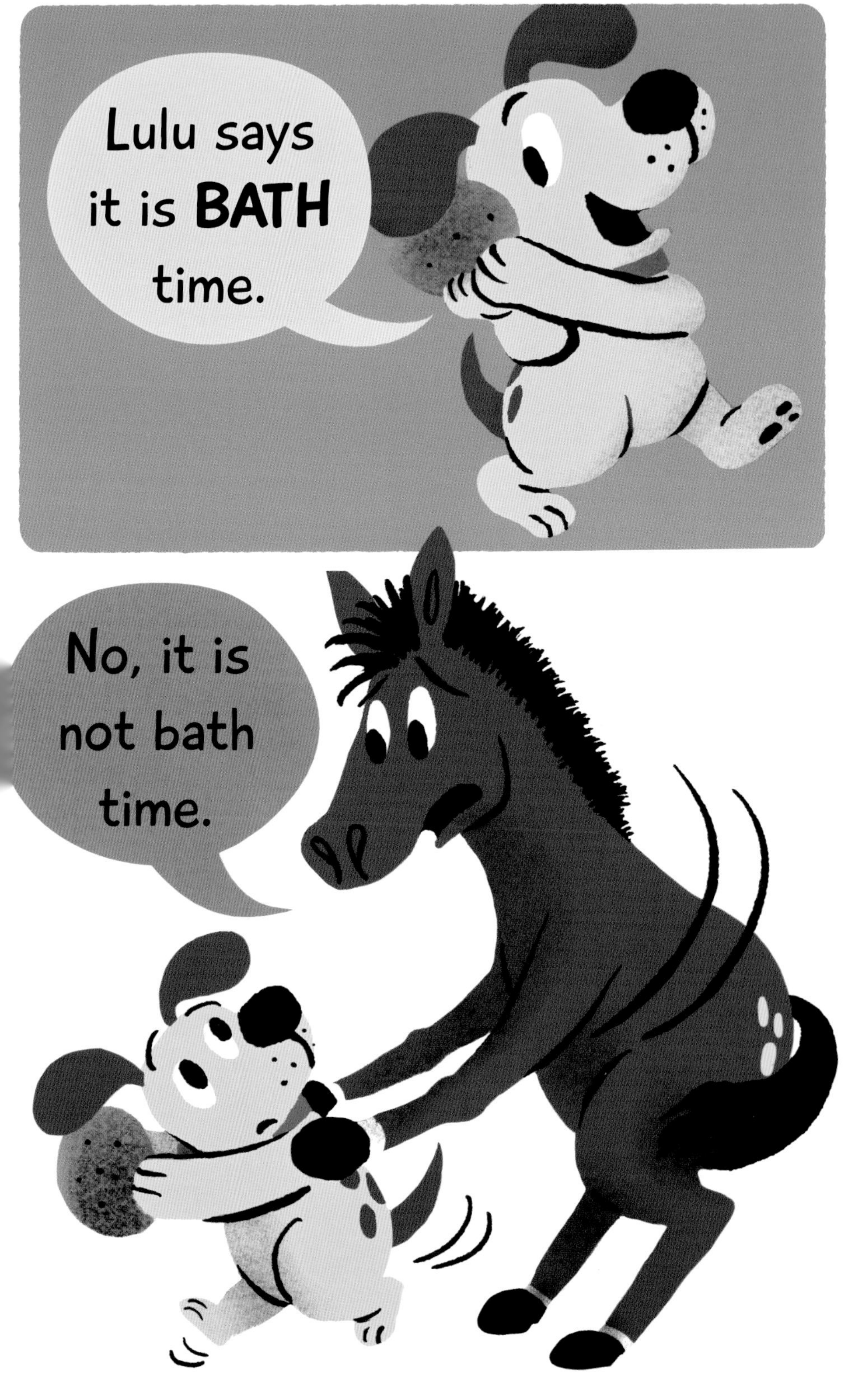
Lulu says it is **BATH** time.
No, it is not bath time.

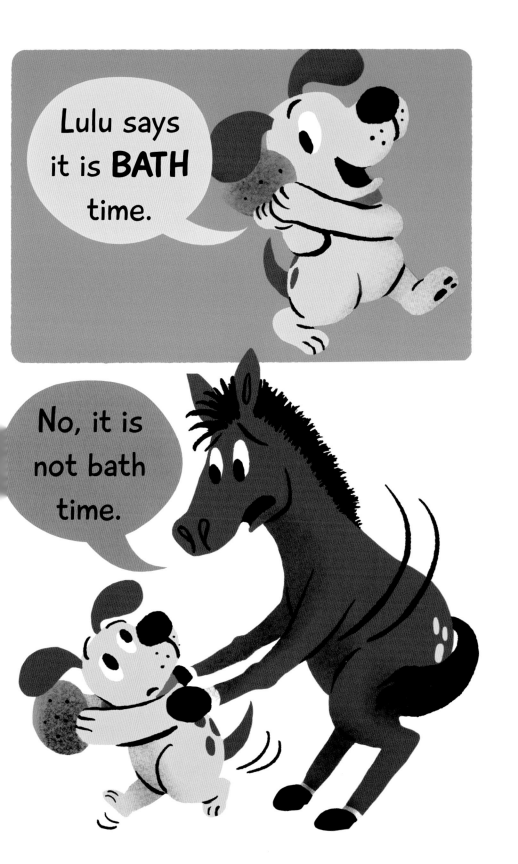

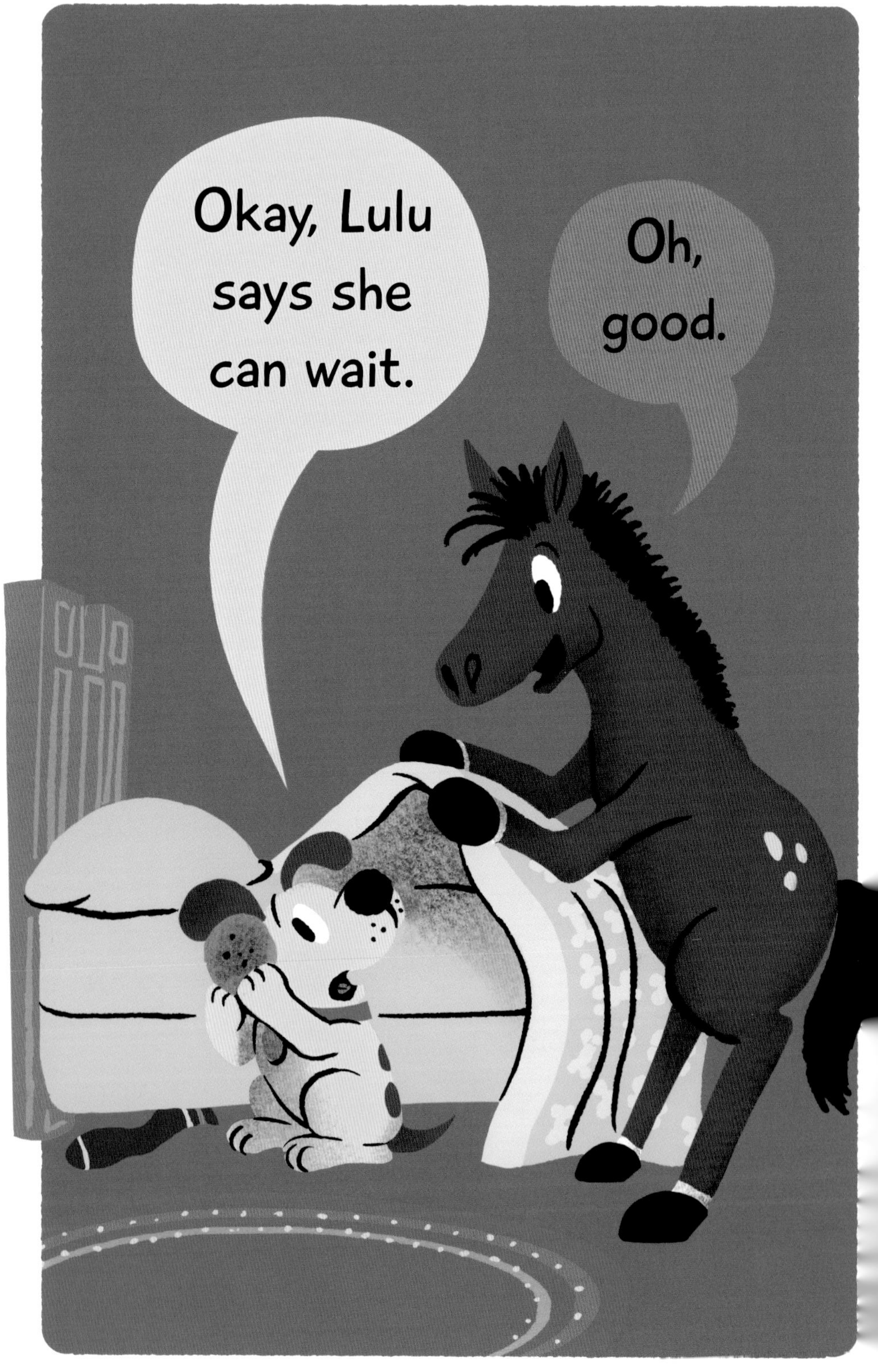
Okay, Lulu says she can wait.
Oh, good.

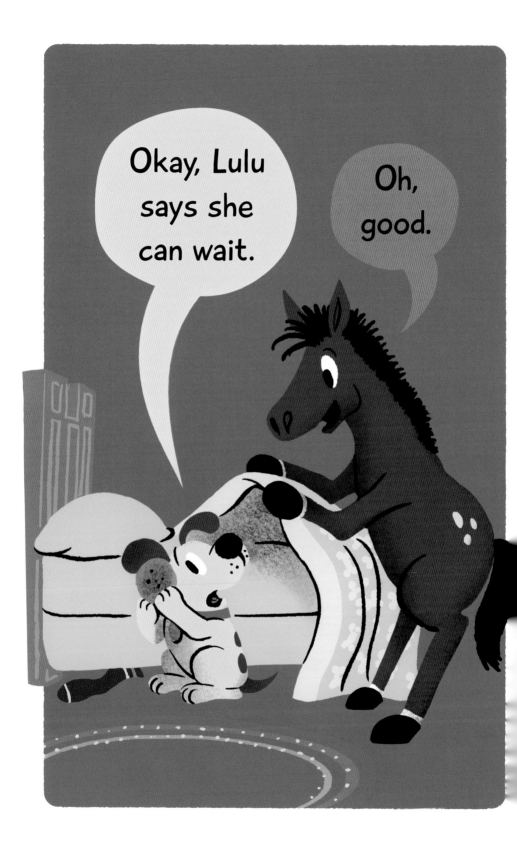

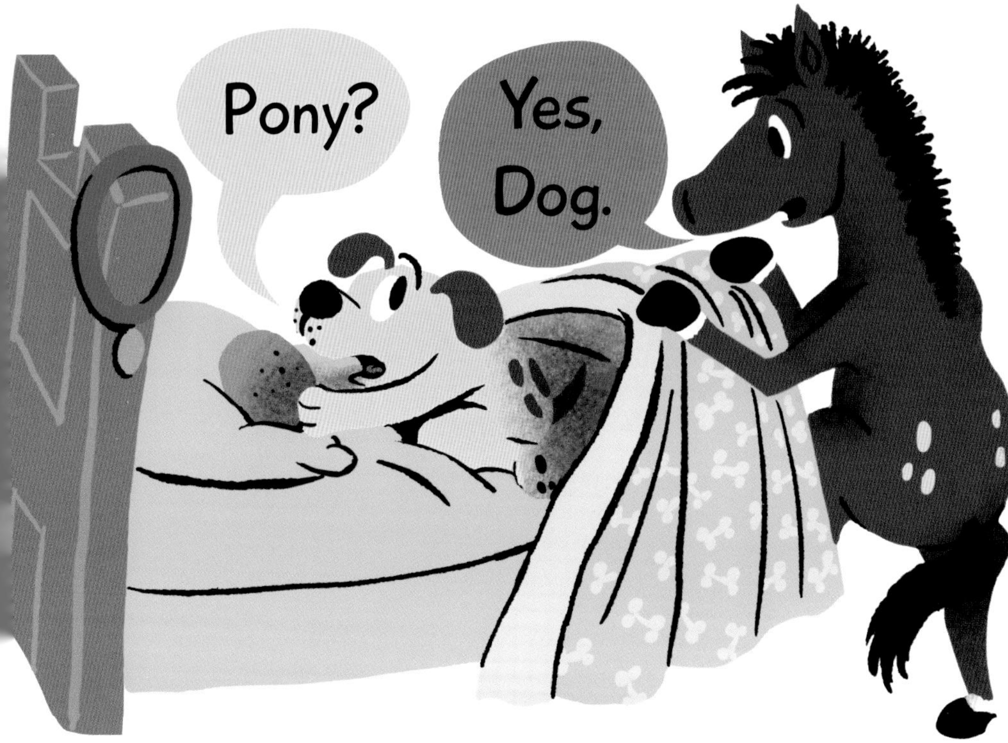
Pony?
Yes, Dog.

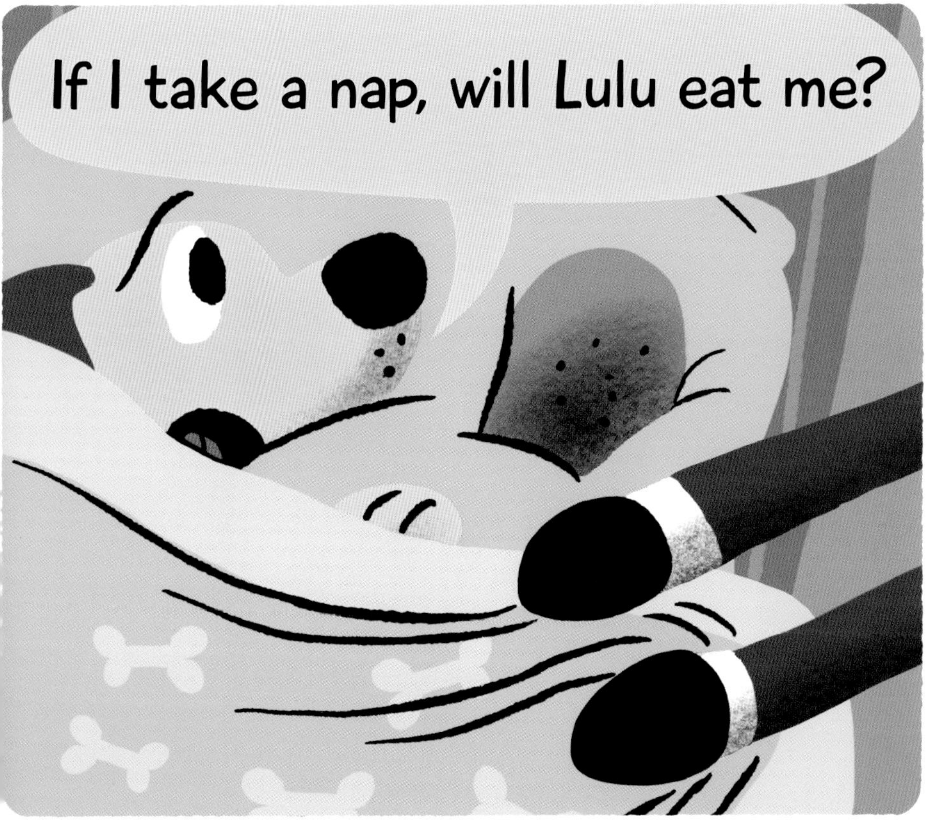
If I take a nap, will Lulu eat me?

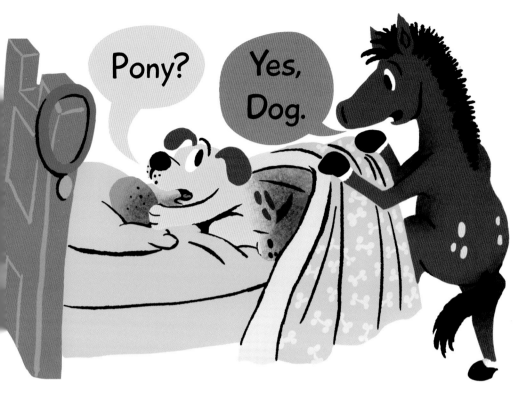

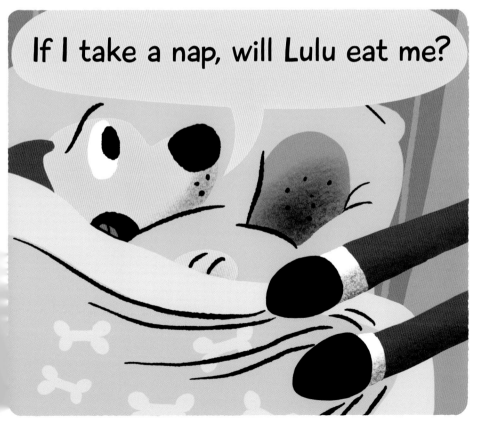

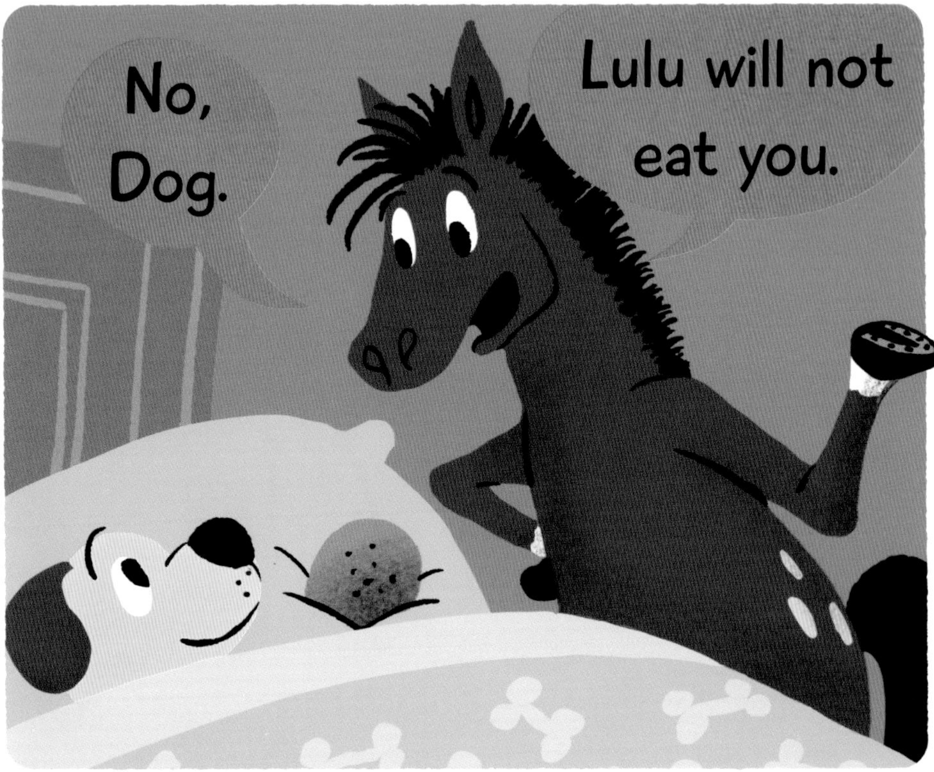
No,
Dog.
Lulu will not
eat you.

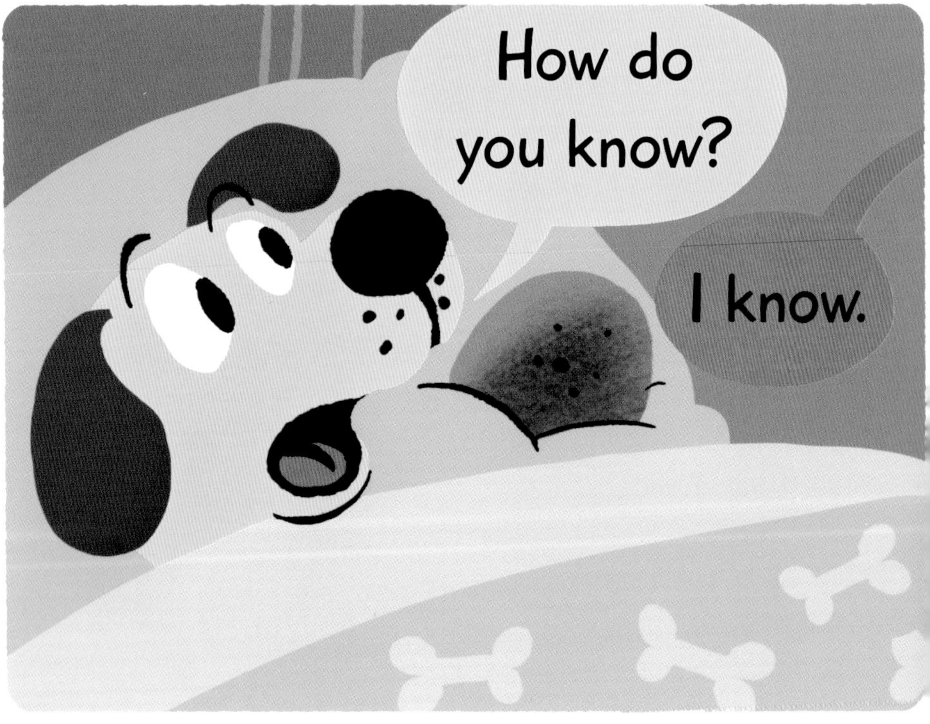
How do
you know?
I know.

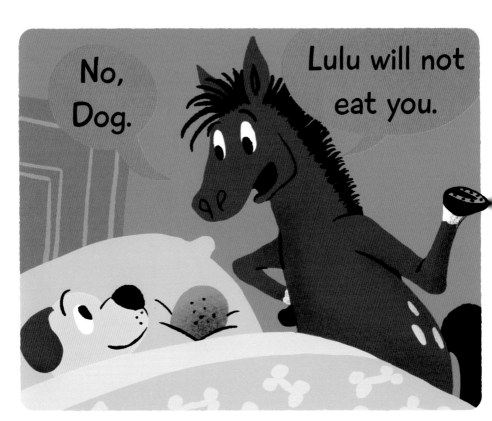

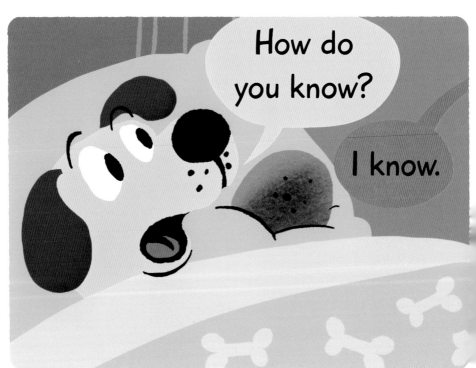

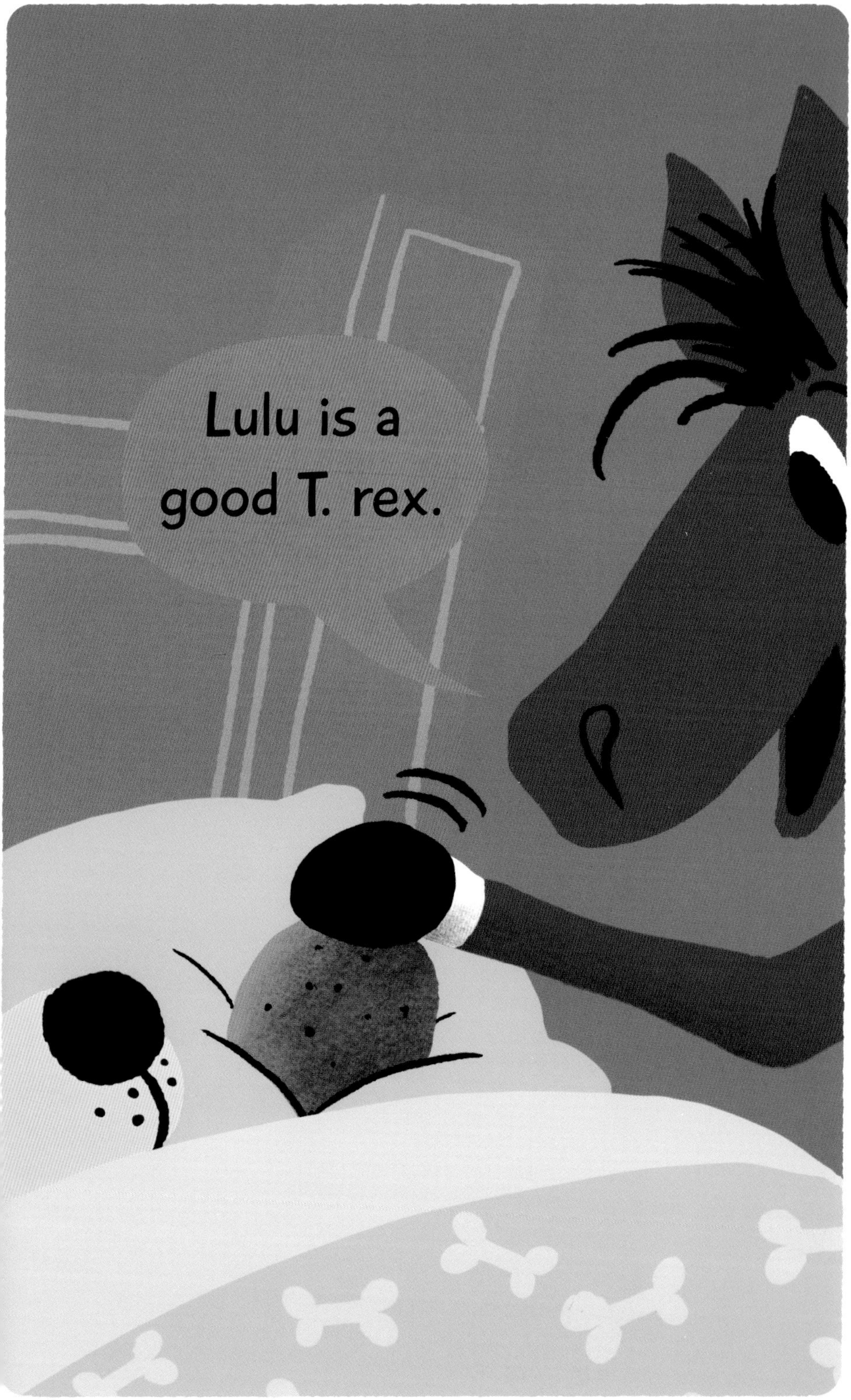
Lulu is a good T. rex.

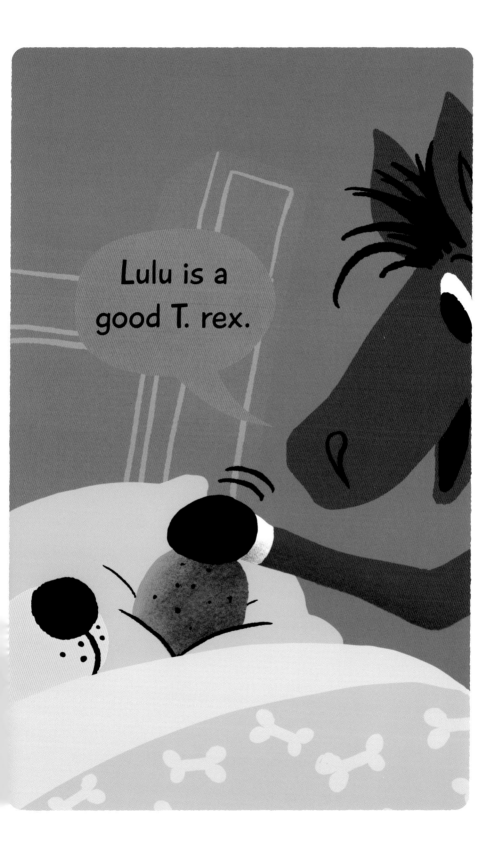

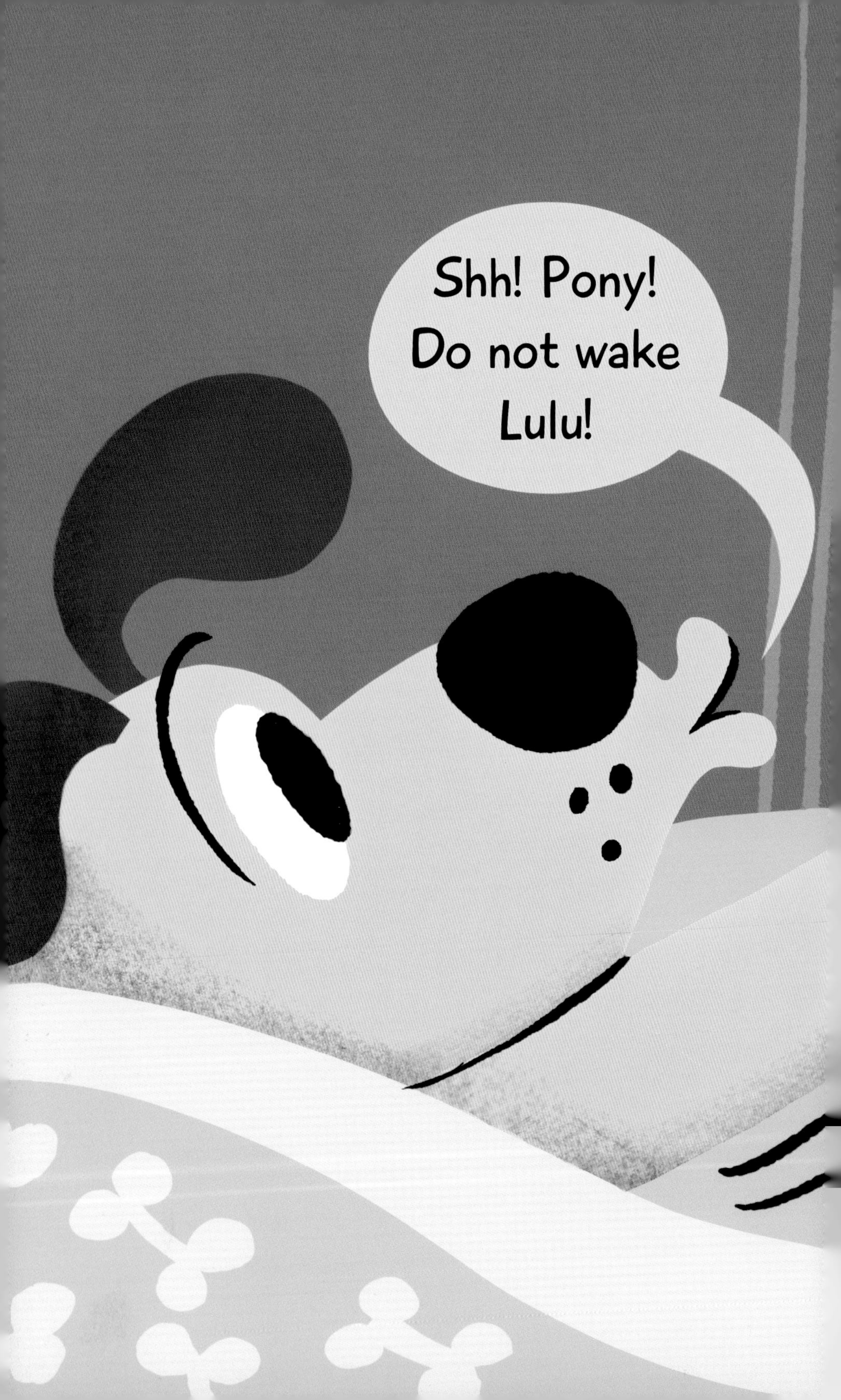
Shh! Pony! Do not wake Lulu!

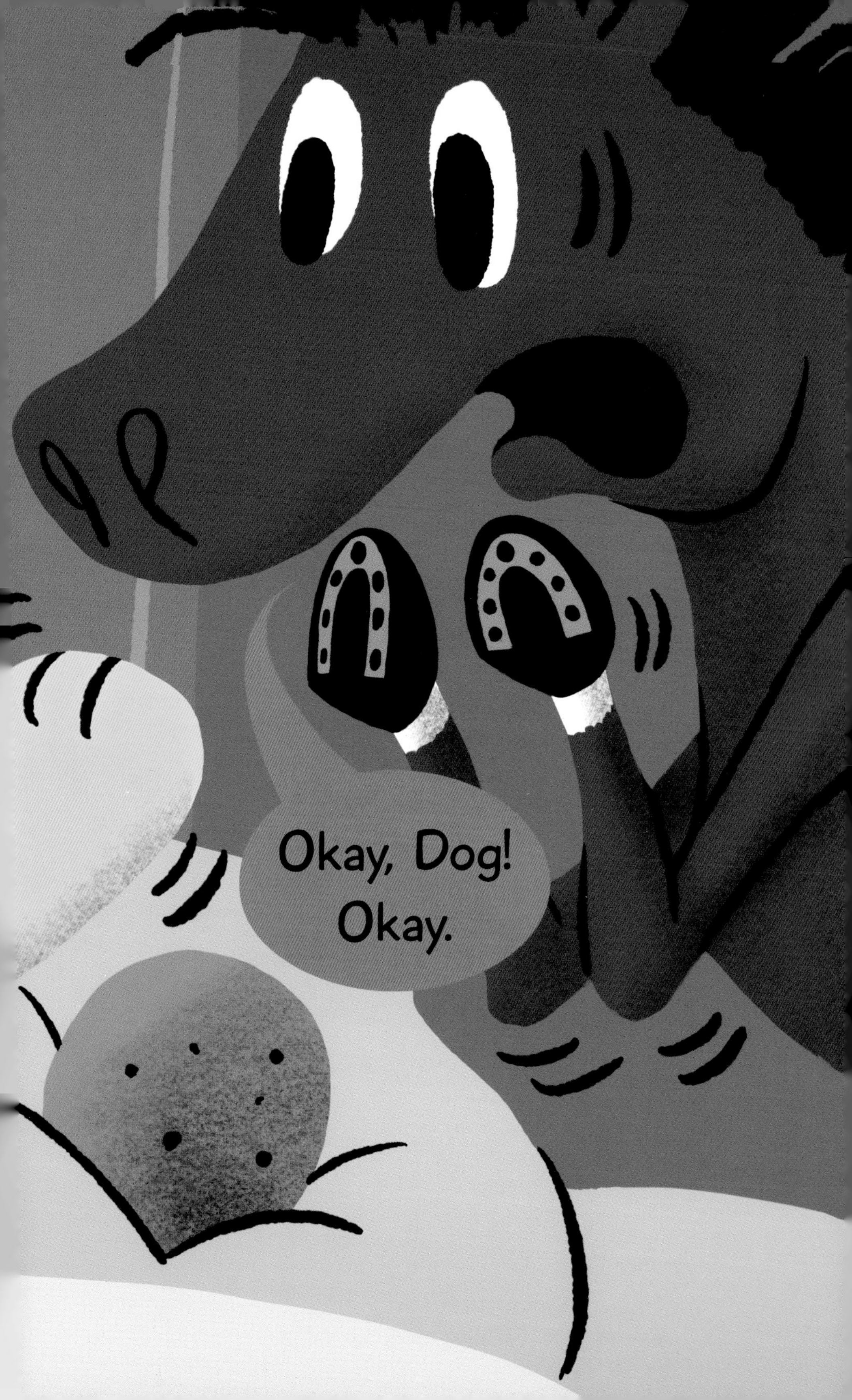
Okay, Dog! Okay.

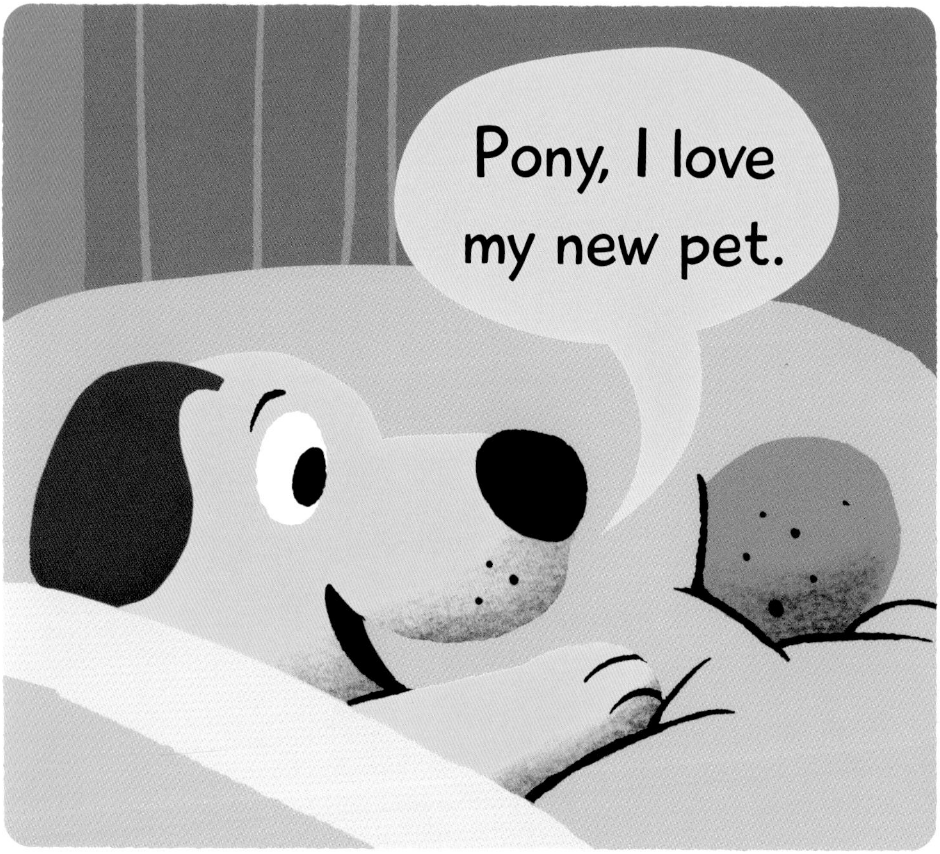
Pony, I love my new pet.

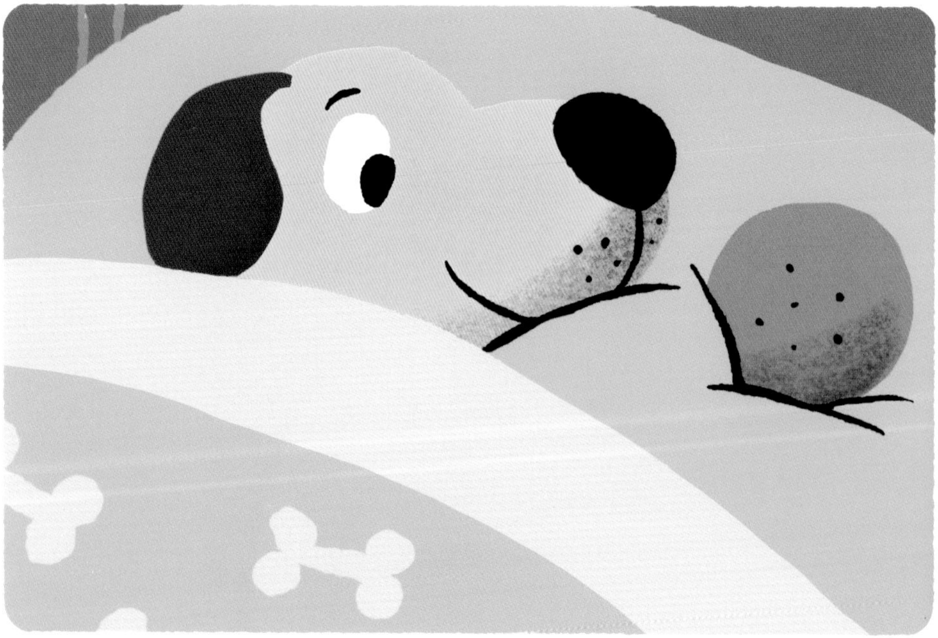

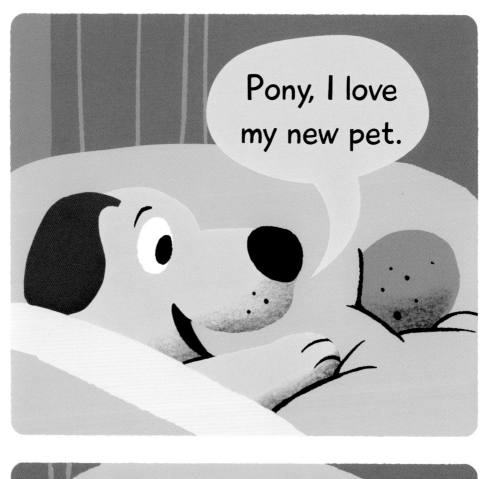

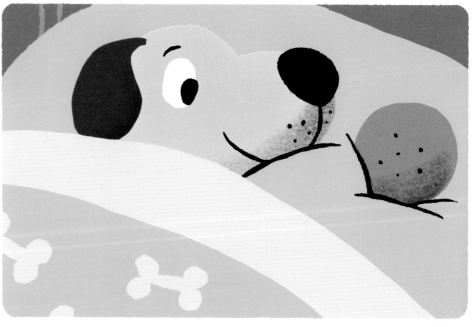

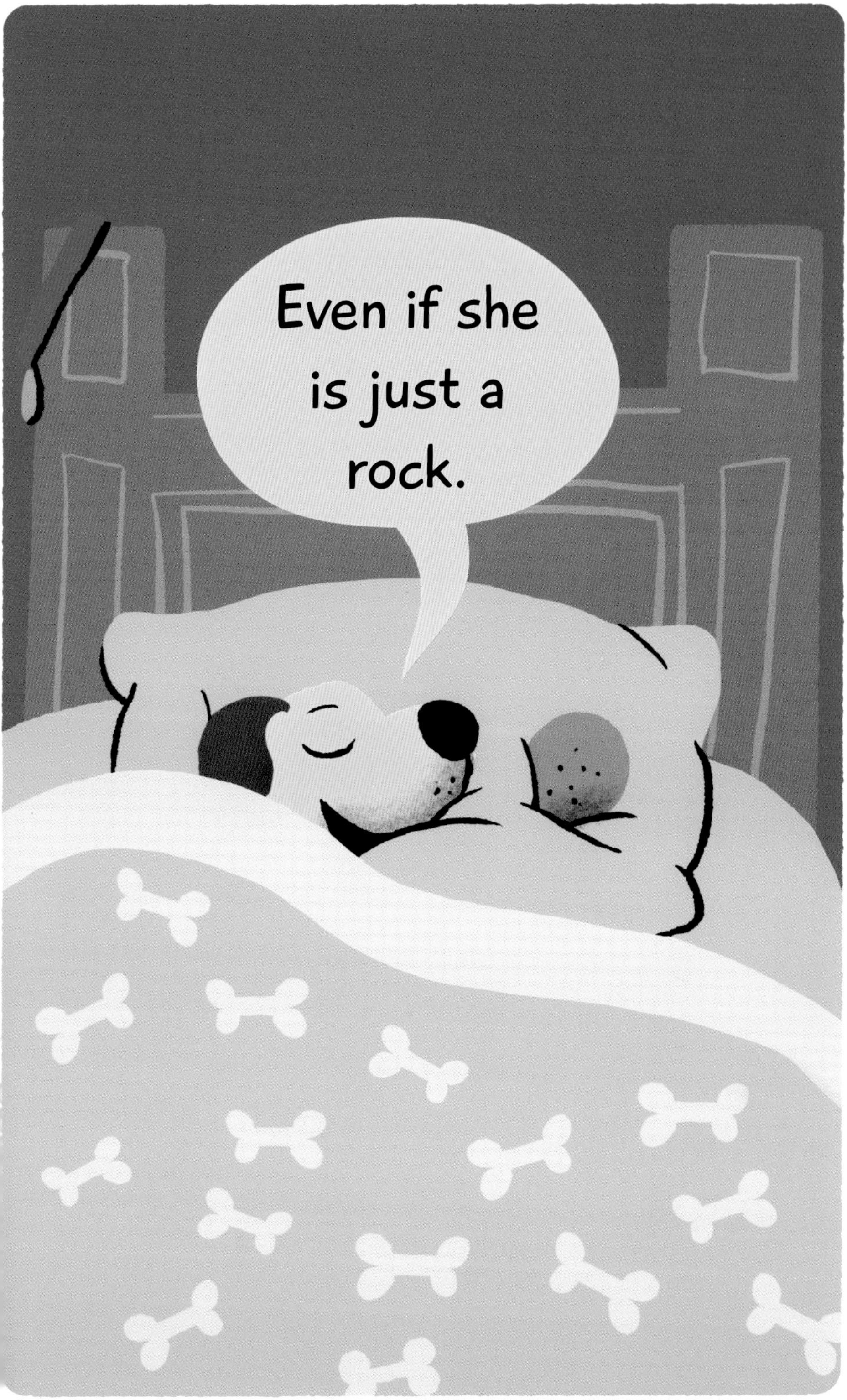
Even if she is just a rock.

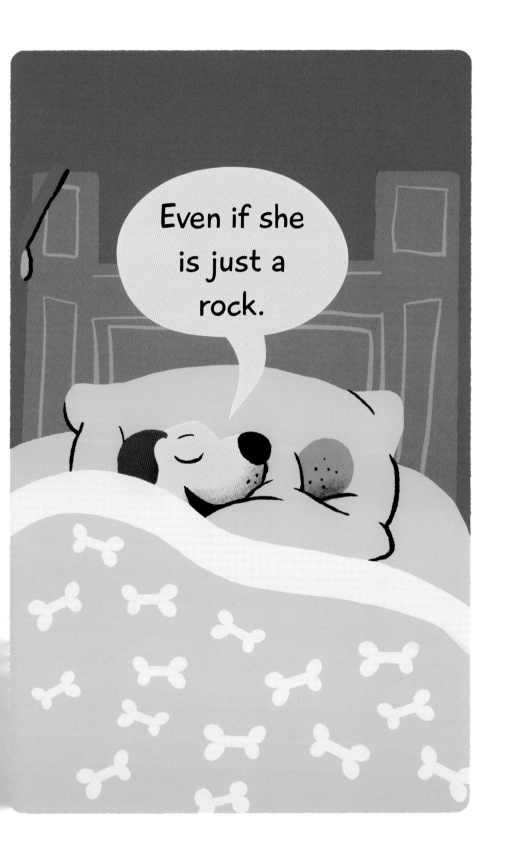

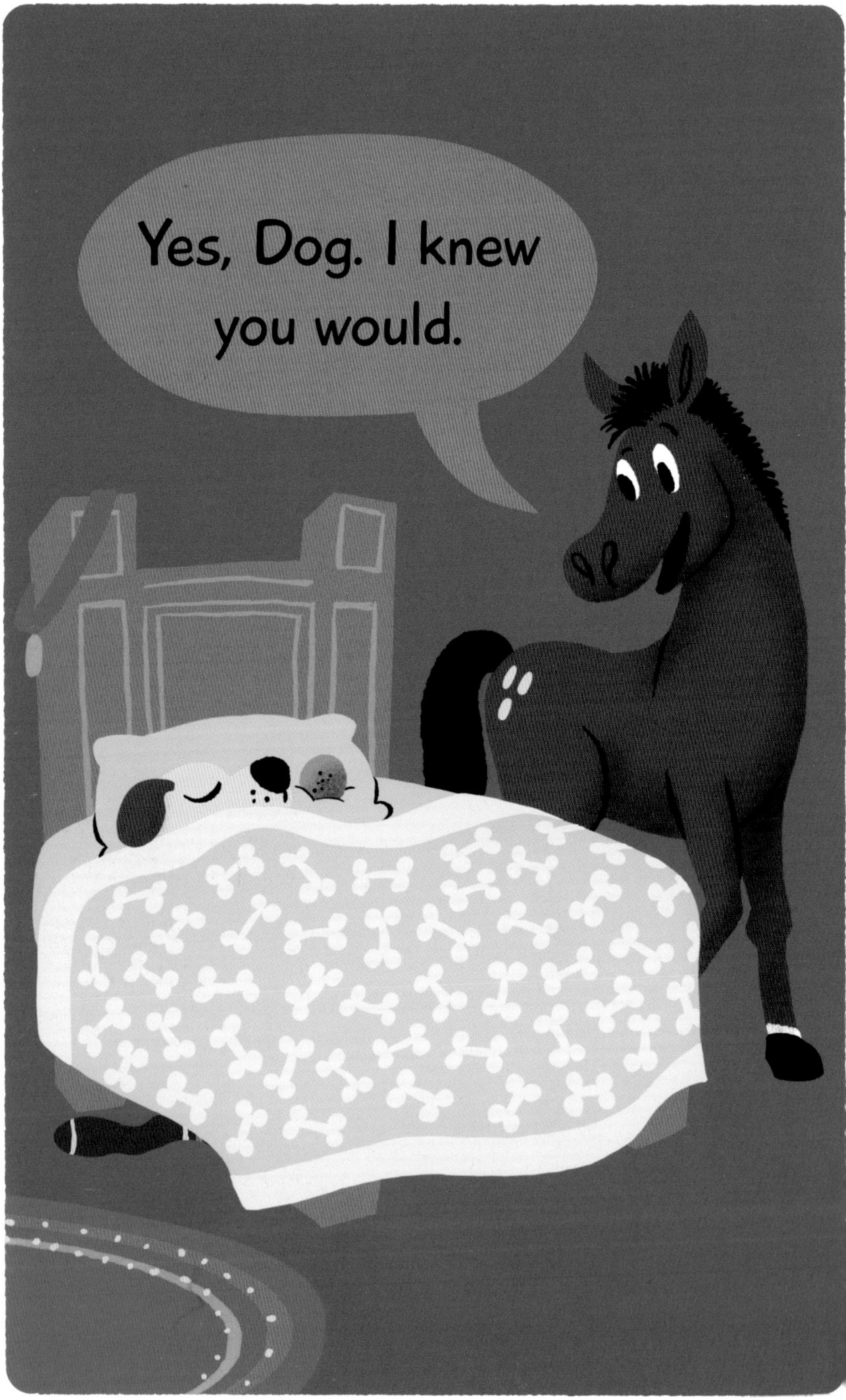
Yes, Dog. I knew you would.

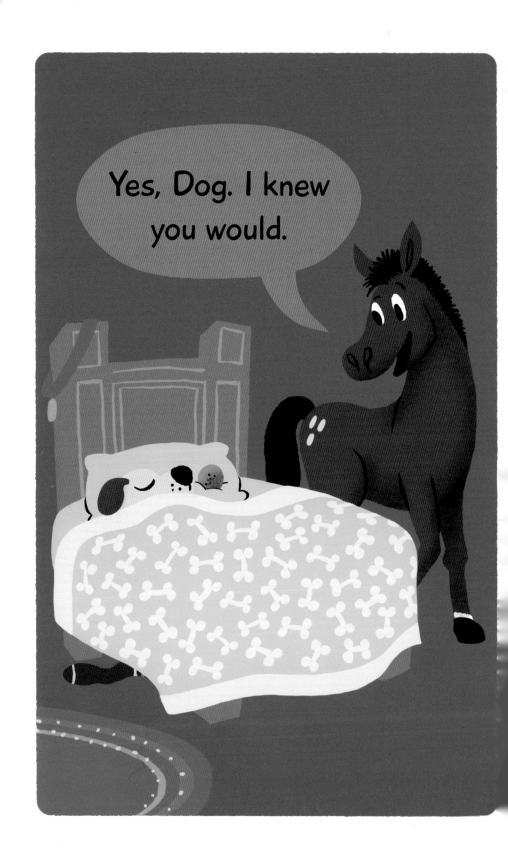